STARTING FROM HAPPY

PATRICIA MARX

A NOVEL

WITH ILLUSTRATIONS BY THE AUTHOR

SCRIBNER

NEW YORK   LONDON   TORONTO   SYDNEY   NEW DELHI

SCRIBNER
A Division of Simon & Schuster, Inc.
1230 Avenue of the Americas
New York, NY 10020

First Scribner hardcover edition August 2011

SCRIBNER and design are registered trademarks of The Gale Group, Inc., used under license by Simon & Schuster, Inc., the publisher of this work.

For information about special discounts for bulk purchases, please contact Simon & Schuster Special Sales at 1-866-506-1949 or business@simonandschuster.com.

The Simon & Schuster Speakers Bureau can bring authors to your live event. For more information or to book an event contact the Simon & Schuster Speakers Bureau at 1-866-248-3049 or visit our website at www.simonspeakers.com.

Designed by Maura Fadden Rosenthal / Mspace

Manufactured in the United States of America

1   3   5   7   9   10   8   6   4   2

Library of Congress Control Number: 2011010774

ISBN 978-1-4391-0128-5
ISBN 978-1-4391-0995-3 (ebook)

FOR PAUL ROOSSIN

Uh-oh

[Warning: If, in these pages, you encounter an imaginary number or an umlaut, it'll be okay.]

[*Starting from Happy* is composed not of chapters, but of chaplettes. If you are looking for a book with chapters adiós muchachos.]

[Good or bad, something will happen.]

PROLEGOMENON

Philip Roth, after reading an early draft of this book, asked my editor if he could write the foreword. I was encouraged. Not long before the publication had been scheduled to go to press Mr. Roth excused himself from the task, however, reporting that he was obliged to be present at something pastoral.

I was in a quandary. I was under contract to produce a manuscript of a certain length, and had been depending on Roth to bring me to my target word-count. Literature is supposed to be literary, but, as all of us are aware, lawyers not infrequently prevail. Thank goodness Toni Morrison, who'd also been given an advance copy of *Starting from Happy,* said she'd be honored to contribute a prefatory essay. Later that day, she, too, was required to withdraw her offer, implying with great tact, I thought, that Roth had poisoned the well. My editor sent proofs to Joyce Carol Oates. Oates phoned to say that she was sorry but she was suffering from a bout of writer's block.

Cormac McCarthy was under the weather, existentially speaking. Alice Munro was stuck in Manitoba. Margaret Atwood said no—in a spare, enigmatic manner.

John Updike is dead.

Why didn't I, Patricia A. Marx, simply write the front

matter myself? According to my publisher, a foreword is customarily executed by an eminent writer.

I amn't?

I suppose I could have written an opening of some sort—provide the backstory to my novel, say, or explain how it came to be that I wrote this book. But here's the thing. Would that be considered an introduction or a preface? I know that one of those is the one nobody reads, so I'd want to write the other one, the one where you get the lowercase Roman numerals at the bottom of the page. Or do I mean the prologue? Or the epigraph?

I still need either 225 or 227 words—or, rather, two hundred twenty-five or two hundred twenty-seven— depending on how you feel about *uh-oh* (and counting this sentence). Yes, I could've, I mean could have, padded my manuscript—replaced each contraction with the corresponding two words, for instance—but is this the way I want posterity to view my legacy?

Even now, I am at least one hundred and forty-three words shy of the mark.

Bowwow bah bah woof ribbit ribbit meow moo coo roar.

Caw to-keh gobble gobble quack quack quack.

Neigh.

Cheep cluck buzz grrr chatter gibber cluck hiss whoop.

Chirrup oink squawk cock-a-doodle-doo.

Moo coo bark bark woof bah bah bgirk bruk bruk bruk.

Woof chatter.

Meow roar quack quack warble to-keh gobble gobble gibber growl.

Scram.

Bleat whiny grunt night cheep arg cluck buzz grrr.

Gibber cluck caw quack hiss whoop.

Low chirrup squawk caw oink oink blub glug swish squeak eek.

Polly want a cracker?

Croak cuckoo mew bell trumpet moan drone cackle pitter.

Click pipe whistle scram gobble gobble.

Crow bellow yelp moo squeak squeal arf growl purr.

Trumpet chant eek baa buzz fink scram.

Howl honk.

Melba toast.

Oink neigh oink.

Hoo-hoo do you think you are jug-gug howl snort.

Hee-haw.

WHO'S WHO

(in order of appearance, except when not)

IMOGENE GILFEATHER: Lingerie designer. Likes things just so. Pet peeves: everything. Not her real hair color.

WALLY YEZ: Scientist whose field of study Patty does not understand. Knows a lot of things. Hates fake crap. Likes real crap. Wishes *upside-down* was one word.

PATTY: Author. Tried to be omniscient, but kept forgetting things.

RON DE JEAN: Sleep researcher. Married, if you can call it that. Patty tried to like him. Still trying.

GWEN DWORKIN: Shared a house with Wally—also a turtle and a piece of taffy. As a child, used to break into friends' houses and refold their towels. Highest IQ in this book—next to Patty's, of course.

HARRIET: Imogene's assistant. From New Orleans, but talks normal because accents too time-consuming to write and read.

MEG AND RICHARD SEPKOWITZ: Accountants known for their sprightly, tax-deductible dinner parties.

Not particularly known for anything else. Neither can tolerate the numeral 9.

DEREK: Wally's best friend. Uneasy with any food that is toasted. On deathbed, finally forgave author for failing to give him a last name.

ERNA GILFEATHER: Imogene's mother. Has no wrinkles, the result of her having committed early on to a life without smiling. Divides her time between being glad she brought a sweater and wishing she'd brought a sweater.

BEENISH ASIF: Seems to have her sights set on Wally. Outgoing phone machine says, "This is Beenish. If you pay for it, I'll eat it."

DONALD CHARM: Senior lingerie buyer at Saks Fifth Avenue. Wears a preponderance of argyle and lives with a mother-doll. Taciturn in twelve languages.

STUFFY: Endangered. Update: dead.

ELSIE EVANGELISTA: Wally's barber. Her word against ours. Packages sent to Elsie always returned to sender.

BOUNCE: Until age four, thought he was age six. At age six, thought he was five. At age five, thought he was a subway car on the Lexington Avenue line.

LINLIN: Only flaw is her perfection.

UXUE: Bounce's sweetheart. Her name is consistently misspelled in these pages, possibly on this one as well.

IGOR FLATEV: Broke LinLin's heart. Is anagram for "I love graft."

LEONARD: A minor character who slept his way into this book. With Gwen.

MRS. DEEDEE DOE: Litigant. Never knew what hit her.

MISSY WINKELMAN: Next-door neighbor. Don't get me started. . . .

PAUL S. ROOSSIN: God only knows.

 : A kumquat.

START HERE

1.

It did not, as a matter of fact, start from happy for either of them. Imogene Gilfeather had just had a cruel haircut and for this reason, or maybe another, expressed little interest that night when the fellow sitting next to her on the bus down Broadway said he knew the perfect guy for her.

"Perfect," said Imogene Gilfeather, "is not my type."

2.

The perfect guy was Wally Yez. As Imogene Gilfeather was rejecting Wally Yez sight unseen, Wally's beloved pet black squirrel was being electrocuted. The rodent, it seems, had ventured onto the amateur radio antenna that Wally had set up on his roof, most likely amateurishly.

Bereavement notwithstanding, Wally Yez was intrigued when, the next day, a guy at the hardware store, a friend of a friend of an acquaintance, asked if Wally would like to meet a certain Imogene Gilfeather. What intrigued Wally most? Not that Imogene Gilfeather had a one-and-a-half-bedroom with a wraparound terrace or that she knew how to make éclairs or that she was available. What intrigued Wally most about Imogene Gilfeather was that she designed a line of lingerie. It was called Featherware.

"Damn," Wally said, wishing he had not gone in with

Gwen on the dual membership to the American Museum of Natural History. Wally was a big believer in devotion. Then Wally remembered that the membership was a promotional offer, good for only three months.

3.

There will be no representations of underwear, not even long johns, in *Starting from Happy*.* Patty** is far too demure to enter into a realm so salacious. Nor will she pander to the oglers or the shoppers. Also, she wouldn't know how to begin to draw a brassiere. Instead of Featherware, then: a cactus, of the utmost propriety.

4.

Wally and Gwen renewed their dual membership to the American Museum of Natural History. Every so often, it

---

*A bare-faced lie. See pages 25, 95, and 155.
**Patty.

crossed Wally's mind: Would there come a time when he and Gwen would upgrade to the family membership?

Wally took Gwen to a swank supper club on the river to celebrate the seven-month anniversary of their first meal together. While the band played a melancholy "Can't Buy Me Love," Wally presented Gwen with a locket. In the candlelight, Gwen read aloud the inscription on the gold-plated heart: "Twenty-five Beautiful Years Together. Norman and Arlene."

"Whoops," said Wally, promising to pick up the correct necklace in the morning, and then Wally and Gwen shared a tepid laugh.

WALLY'S GUIDE to ANNIVERSARY GIFTS

Foam	Concrete	Velour	Steel Wool or Lint
1st	2nd	5th	9th
Shoelaces	Schmutz	Wax	Quintessence
13th	15th	20th	25th
graft	Plutonium	Brochure	Rubbish
30th	45th	50th	60th

Wally also gave Gwen a lifetime membership to the New York City Police Museum. "A lady from the Widows' and Children's Benefit Fund called, and how could I hurt her feelings?" said Wally.

Gwen gave Wally a scale for the bathroom.

5.

The next day, Wally stood on the scale because there was no room in the bathroom to stand anywhere else. Wally wasn't feeling too hot, owing perhaps to the hollandaise sauce at the swank supper club. Hollandaise sauce or no hollandaise sauce, Gwen insisted on Wally's attendance at the going-away clambake that afternoon for the old man who cleaned the pipettes in Gwen and Wally's lab.

In the apple pie line at the clambake, Wally was introduced to one of the big deals in sleep disorder research, Dr. Ron de Jean (pronounced first like the Kurosawa film, and then like the mustard), and also to his date. "I know who you are," Dr. Ron de Jean's date said to Wally as soon as she heard his name. "You are the man I was supposed to marry." She was Imogene Gilfeather.

"And you," said Wally, "are the woman who . . ." He was going to say something about undergarments, but instead he said, ". . . and you are the woman who makes soufflés." She did not look like a woman who specialized in lace or egg whites, thought Wally. Tall and thin, with jutting cheeks and fiery red hair, she looked like a kitchen match that stubbornly would not light. If Imogene produced a culinary pièce de résistance, Wally guessed it would be an orange-ginger vinaigrette or maybe a watercress sandwich with the crusts intact.

"Soufflés?" Imogene said. "I am not insouciant enough for soufflés." Had this comment been devised to beguile? Patty does not know. Wally was, nonetheless, beguiled. He watched Imogene tilt her head forward and rearrange her hair into a high ponytail.

6.

But Wally, you may remember, was a big believer in devotion. He and Gwen said their adieus to the host and hostess. That night the four winds blew fiercely through their bedroom.

7.

Imogene Gilfeather and Ron de Jean removed themselves from the going-away clambake before coffee and taffy were served. Ron was eager to return to his lab to see if any of the subjects had woken up while he was gone. Imogene was antsy, too. She had been seized with an idea for a new bustier while chatting with the guy whose shirt was not tucked in (Wally). Imogene wanted to go home and make a sketch before she forgot where to put the snaps.

The taxi pulled up to Imogene's. "Might be able to squeeze in a few minutes," Ron de Jean said. Not much later, he said, "Sorry I can't stay longer. Can you help me buckle my belt?"

"Why is it that men always assume women want them to spend the night?" Imogene said, but Ron did not hear her say it.

HOW TO TAKE OFF
YOUR 36-HOUR FEATHERWARE PUZZLE BRA

STEP 1

Questions to ask yourself:

"Do I really want to take it off?"

"Has it been on for at least 36 hours?"

"Who am I?"

STEP 2

Find a mirror in a darkened room

room →

STEP 3

Remove all sharp objects, including hat pins, brooches, razor blades, and...

Spontoons

STEP 4

Take phone off hook.

STEP 5

get small piece of plastic tubing in case of breathing emergency

STEP 6

Do 20 minutes of stretching exercises. (Recent research indicates this may increase likelihood of injury.)

STEP 7

Maneuver into the Thirsty Camel position.

STEP 8

No! That's the Leaping Llama position.

STEP 1

If strap 3b (see diagram 6d) will not loop over head, remove left arm.

8.

By the time Ron de Jean was in the elevator, Imogene had roughed out a sketch of the bustier with snaps, and thrown it away, deciding it looked like a jerkin for a toddler or a peanut costume. By the time Ron de Jean was in the lobby, Imogene had put on the teakettle and Billie Holiday and taken off her mascara and being-with-someone face.

Imogene scrolled through her e-mail. Ninety-seven of them—most from friends, a few from rayon and Lycra vendors, three identical messages from someone named Mirilla Borth promising her a job in the Turkmenistan diplomatic corps, and one from Saks Fifth Avenue which filled her with hope that the chain might one day carry Featherware.

9.

Imogene looked around the living room/dining alcove and beheld her art nouveau fireplace with art deco fireplace accessories; her Serapi carpet with an unusual spider design and an extensive use of teal; her collection of miniature stone fruit that included a rare half kumquat; her nineteenth-century dining room table, perfectly distressed; her books (arranged alphabetically); her snuff bottle collection (arranged snuffily); her flattering lighting system (installed by a leading man in the field of illumination); her piece of Australian aboriginal art snagged on a trip to Oceania (and artfully positioned on the wall by a framer friend); and, of course, her wraparound terrace (which added significant value to her one-and-one-half-bedroom co-op with paid-off mortgage). She contemplated her Indian jasper countertop in the kitchen, her linen closet with French fabrics in the hallway, her impressive water pressure in the bathroom, and her nice big television in the bedroom.

She marveled that, an enviable social calendar notwithstanding, she would be free this night and could do what she pleased.

She was thankful that nobody was there to catch the sight of her in her excruciatingly comfortable sweatpants as she ate steamed broccoli from a big plastic tub.

10.

Imogene considered how great it was she'd never run anyone over.

11.

She thought, "My, my, I am happy!"

12.

One fine day, Imogene frantically watched as her laptop slid into a public toilet owing to the demise of its carrying case's tragically frayed shoulder strap. Afterward, the computer would no longer boot up, and when it struggled to come to life, Imogene could make out the puk-a-yuk puk-a-yuk of a distant outboard motorboat. Or perhaps the ghost of plumbing past. Yet Imogene had faith that experts could fix everything.

She called the technical support hotline, two dollars and fifty cents a half-minute, including the time it takes the expert to check the serial number and validate the warranty. Thirteen dollars into the conversation: "May I ask you a personal question?" said the female expert on the other end of the technical support hotline. Imogene prepared herself to state her mother's maiden name.

"Are you on medication?" the expert said.

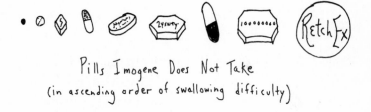

Pills Imogene Does Not Take
(in ascending order of swallowing difficulty)

13.

It was times like these that Imogene wished she had had children, because surely by now one of them would be eleven and therefore old enough to fix her computer.

Ron de Jean might possibly have been of help, but he was in Wilkes-Barre, Pennsylvania, at an antibedwetting convention.

It was times like these that Imogene wished someone would tell her what to do or, better yet, do it for her.

It was times like these that Imogene could have had a stiff drink, popped a pill, joined a cult, sweetened the pot, paid someone off, double-crossed her family (if it would have made a difference), found religion, made a deal with the devil, moved to a faraway place, stayed under the covers, cried a river, crumpled into a teeny ball, thrown a tantrum, had a stroke, hollered and hollered and hollered and hollered some more.

14.

But Imogene wasn't the type.

15.

Wally Yez's business card, which Imogene had recently found in a pocketbook she hadn't carried since God-knows-when, said "An Answer for Everything." Wally Yez? Didn't ring a bell. Still, she thought, it was worth a try. Wasn't everything?

Imogene hoped Wally Yez wasn't the chiropractor she'd sat next to at the Sepkowitzes' party—the guy who believed the secrets of the universe were contained in the alignment of the spine and also creamed corn.

Step 2.

Throw away this
portion of paper.

16.

When the phone rang, Wally had been crimping the origami paper he needed to put the finishing touches on the bony tail and massive knob plate of an ankylosaurid dinosaur. "I remember you" was what Wally said when Imogene telephoned. "You're the girl who practically proposed to me in the apple pie line."

Imogene started to wonder:

Could this guy be a crack? But, as anyone who has ever needed a favor knows, you make allowances.

Step 1.

Cut along dotted line to form
Origami — Approved (OA) Square

Step 3.

Fold so "crack"
is over "But."

17.

"Can I be blunt?" Wally Yez said over the telephone to Imogene Gilfeather. No further words were needed to convey to Imogene that the prognosis regarding her computer and possibly everything else was not propitious.

"Mind if we skip the part of the conversation in which you tell me in stern tones that I should have backed up my files?" said Imogene. "And certainly let's not waste time reflecting upon the lesson I learned the hard way."

"I understand," said Wally, going straight to the part of the conversation in which he asked, "Are you still with Don le Juan?"

"Ron de Jean?" said Imogene. "Not really. He's sort of with someone." By *someone,* Imogene meant his wife. By *sort of,* Imogene meant sort of.

Wally asked Imogene if she would like to accompany him this weekend to a hootenanny upstate.

"Weekend?! Hootenanny?! Upstate?!" thought Imogene, and each of those was only one of the reasons she declined.

"What's wrong with dinner in the city?" Imogene said.

"Dinner in the city it is," Wally said. "Pick a night."

"Come to think of it," Imogene said, "I'm not sure it will work. I'm kind of busy with my trunk show and my friend from Brussels will be in town and I'm getting my carpets cleaned and that reminds me, my driver's license is about to expire and, oh, no, I think I meant to make an appointment to see about getting my grandmother's wing chair reupholstered."

What Imogene did not say was that she felt her status quo was sufficiently rich and full. Currently and for the foreseeable future, she had no slots open for Romance.

18.

"What about another night?" said Wally.

19.

Let us now talk about Wally and Gwen. How long were they together? Long enough to put 136,023 miles on one automobile and 47,987 on another. Long enough to acquire a long-haired dachshund puppy who grew up and gave birth to a litter of long-haired dachshund puppies. Long enough to buy a house in the suburbs together. Long enough to agree it is silly to celebrate one more Valentine's Day when they could put the money they'd have spent into a fund set aside to remodel the kitchen. Long enough to fire two contractors. Long enough for the third contractor to misunderstand Gwen and chop down Wally's favorite tree on Arbor Day. Long enough for Gwen to have heard all of Wally's best stories and not hesitate to interrupt him when she felt she could tell one in a more entertaining way than he could. Long enough for Wally to marvel at how he had never tired of Gwen's anecdote about the 1955 penny and the milkshake. Long enough for both of them to say some fairly beastly things about each other's family. Long enough for Wally to give up short-sleeved shirts because of Gwen's conviction that only butchers wear short-sleeved shirts. Long enough for Gwen to wear her dental night guard to bed. Long enough for Gwen to reach the conclusion that a king-size bed wouldn't be such a bad idea. Long enough for Wally to agree it wouldn't. Long enough for Wally and Gwen to hold dual memberships to museums in three states, the District of Columbia, and the

Netherlands, but not long enough for them to view any art or artifacts. Long enough to fill a Dumpster with their stuff after they sold the house in the suburbs. Long enough for their dachshund to have a hip replacement and die.

Long enough for Patty to be glad she's not Wally and Gwen.

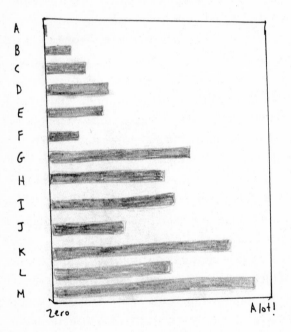

Duration of Wally & Gwen's Coupledom:
How Does It Compare?

A=Wally and Gwen.
B=Longest amount of time, in eons, a sinner in Limbo has waited to enter Heaven.
C=Shortest time, in epochs, a customer calling AT&T has been put on hold.
D=Number of incidents last year when a human being was mistaken for a penguin.

E=Hours it takes to pan-roast a fully grown penguin.

F=Time, in years, it takes for raw meat in freezer to sprout florets.

G=Days Austin Gillespie stayed home from first grade because he said his stomach hurt from global warming.

H=Dollars, in trillions, of rewards promised in e-mails supposedly originating in Nigeria.

I=Annual requests on death row for steak, fries, and a side of Pileggi.

J=Percentage of Norwegians who deliberately give lost foreigners incorrect directions.

K=Percentage of movie characters who cough in first act and die in third act.

L=Number of times the words *verily* and *beget* are used erroneously in the Bible.

M=Time, in weeks, it took Patty to draw this graph.

20.

At the point that Wally asked Imogene to the hootenanny, Hurricane Gwen and Typhoon Wally had made landfall in the rec room, also known as the basement.

21.

"Let me get this straight," said Elsie Evangelista, "she turns the hootenanny down and a few days later, you ask her to a magic show?"

"The lumbosacral region. There! Rub there," said Wally.

"She must think you're twelve," said Elsie.

"Trust me," said Wally. "Women cannot resist Wally Yez."

"Uh-huh," said Elsie.

"Haven't I always had a girlfriend?" said Wally. "I've always had a girlfriend since I was fourteen, if you count

Candy Kling letting me touch her bosoms in the cloak-room with the Hornig sisters as witnesses." Wally let his head drop into Elsie's hands.

"Weren't you going to take a breather from the fairer sex?" said Elsie. "Isn't that what you said after you and Gwen split up?"

"I am taking a breather," said Wally. "I told you: Imogene said no."

"Lean your head toward me a little more," said Elsie.

"But she'll say yes eventually," said Wally. "Probably Thursday, if history can tell us anything."

"Further toward me," said Elsie.

"Are you aware," Wally said, "that I've been with you longer than I've been with any other woman?"

(Elsie Evangelista is Wally Yez's hairdresser. They go way back.)

22.

When Wally telephoned to invite Imogene to the Origami Conference in Bridgeport, Imogene was in the middle of designing a piece of stretchy fabric for the prototype of the teddy she wanted to include in the spring collection whose theme was Ancient Egypt.

"What's wrong with a movie?" Imogene said as she scribbled a sacred ibis onto a Chinese take-out menu.

"Too passive," Wally said as he typed Imogene Gilfeather's phone number into his address book.

"If you do not like passive," Imogene said, erasing the ibis's beak, "then you will not like me."

23.

She and Wally settled on a plan to go to a museum and dinner, but not for three weeks because Imogene said she could be free no sooner.

(That's what she said. Patty's seen Imogene's calendar, however, and wants to know: since when does "get super to change lightbulb" constitute being busy?)

"Have you ever been to Larry's French Restaurant?" Wally said. "They have escargots. I know Larry so we could get a good table and some decent gastropods."

"Wherever," said Imogene and then she said goodbye. Wally wrote "Date #1" into a tiny square on his pocket diary.

Imogene returned to Egypt. Truth be told, she did like escargots.

24.

Gwen had quit the lab where she and Wally had worked since they'd met, and would soon be moving down the hall to the insect behavior lab. "But not because of you," she told him the day they got together in the park to decide the fate of their lawn furniture.

"Unlimited number of experimental subjects: all mine to mutilate!" Gwen said. "How could anyone pass up an opportunity like that?" she said.

Wally saw her point. Since their postdoctoral years, he and Gwen had been conducting physiological experiments on animals, including one in which they'd forced cats to listen to Ernest Borgnine's dramatic reading of *Pilgrim's Progress* until their subjects were in no condition to live. Cat lovers were not pleased with this research, and cat lovers, it turned out, have a lot of power to impede shipments of cats (not to mention their influence on what is sold at the cash registers in most bookstores).

"You can have the furniture," Wally said.

"Why don't you take it?" said Gwen. "I don't have a house."

"Neither do I," said Wally. The house they each didn't have was, of course, the same house, their having sold it the other day to a man who planned to start a family as soon as he could find a woman to start one with.

"There's something I need to talk to you about," said Gwen.

"Should we sit down?" said Wally as he sat down on a bench.

"I'm pregnant," said Gwen, who had remained standing.

"Is that possible?" said Wally. "I mean it's absolutely wonderful, but you know what I mean." Wally stood up. If he were going to be a father, it behooved him, he felt, to be as tall as he could be.

Gwen sat down.

"It's not only possible," said Gwen, "it's doubly possible." Gwen saw the confusion or something else in Wally's eyes. "I sort of was having a thing with Leonard," she said.

"Leonard in the lab?" said Wally.

25.

Wally asked himself how he could have spent so many years with a girl like this and why he would not have been unhappy to spend some more years with her had she not dumped him. Or had he dumped her, he wondered. If he does not know, how can we?

26.

Gwen was pregnant and then she was not. In both cases, it was never clear how it had happened.

27.

Imogene was young and then she was old. She could not tell you how this had happened, but she had a needling feeling that it might have been her fault. Should she have been using night cream all these years? Eaten more salmon? Been a life-long devotee of yoga? No, thought Imogene, nobody could blame her for not doing yoga. They hadn't invented yoga when she was a spring chicken, had they? What about those flax pills that her friend Joie Finkelstein swears by? No, they wouldn't have preserved her: has anybody taken a good look at Joie Finkelstein lately? Perhaps if she had listened to the radio more often, tuned into the young people's stations—would a little bit of youth have worn off on her? Imogene felt rueful that she had not been more conscientious about sleep and she worried she shouldn't have been so worried all the time.

Was it possible Imogene had received a letter when she was in her twenties, asking her to check a box if she wanted to stay young? Just like me, thought Imogene, to forget to open a letter like that.

Most of the time, Imogene did not feel old. Her bones felt the way she remembered them always feeling, if one can remember such a thing. She did not wear dirndls or velour tunics or baggy pants with elastic waistbands (except at night). No. She wore halter tops on occasion and had a streak in her hair. Girls half her age could not walk in her shoes, the heels were that high (and no orthotics). Only now and then did she look in the mirror and feel an urgent need to squint.

How old was Imogene? She was thirty-seven. In no time, she was all too well aware, she would surpass the New York State speed limit.

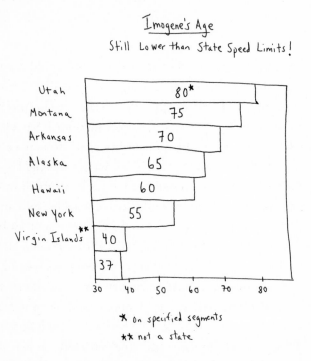

28.

The night of Date #1 was also the night of the First Annual International Silhouette Lingerie Awards, the so-called Nobels of Underwear. Imogene was a finalist in three categories: Best Glamour Nightwear (for her Hepburn Shortie), Best Technical Innovation (for her six-way stretch polyester), and Best Bralette (for her Skim-P).

When Imogene remembered that she'd forgotten about the awards, she telephoned Wally.

"And now for the tip of the day—" Wally's phone machine said. "Don't postpone the joy."

Imogene had been calling to do just that.

29.

Wally was at the lab feeding salty licorice to a cat when Imogene phoned. Imogene was fitting a D+ cover girl when Wally called back.

"D plus," Wally said. "Tell her that if she needs a tutor . . ." Wally had been making a joke and Imogene knew that Wally was making a joke, but Imogene had no time in her life, she believed, for men who made jokes. Nor did she have time for men who bantered, postured, preened, equivocated, explained, chewed the fat, played devil's advocate, watched football, cooked their famous lasagna, explored their feelings, asked her lots of questions, or had too much time.

"Should we come up with another plan?" Imogene said, for Imogene did have time for men with dimples, purpley eyes, rumpled hair, and endearing overbites (if online photos speak the truth). Moreover, she did have time next week. Plus, she felt rotten for canceling on such short notice. "Would next week work?" said Imogene.

"Does this Sunday count as next week?" said Wally.

30.

The First Annual International Silhouette Lingerie Awards was—there is no other word for it—a bust. During the cocktail hour, a certain model, known for her lengthy torso, was arrested in the ladies room for selling ketamine, an anesthetic used in veterinary and human medicine that can have sportive side effects.

The ceremony was . . . well, suffice it to say: first prize for Best T-Shirt Bra went to a Lycra thing designed by FlexCo that nearly everyone agreed belonged in the Shape-wear category. "It is a travesty!" the VIP next to Imogene said as if he'd been sitting not in the McNally Auditorium at Fordham University but in the Peace Palace at the International Court of Justice at The Hague.

Donald Charm, the buyer for Saks Fifth Avenue, did not show up. Given that Imogene won not so much as an Honorable Mention, she was, in point of fact, relieved.

31.

Chaplette 31 is always a difficult chaplette. Let Patty hasten, then, to chaplette 32.

32.

Imogene returned home from the First Annual International Silhouette Lingerie Awards and listened to her voice mail as she kicked off the red strappy sandals, which had been—she hated to admit her mother had been right—

absolutely more suitable than the brown patent leather peep-toes. Imogene turned on the TV, and then called her assistant, Harriet, with an idea for an ethereal chemise line. Imogene was not listening, therefore, when the news anchorman reported that the Special K hustled by the model in the ladies' room at the First Annual International Silhouette Lingerie Awards had been traced to a local vestibulospinal reflexes lab. Wally Yez was a researcher in that lab, but there was no mention of him on the news.

"You think the public is ready for that kind of chemise?" said Harriet on the phone.

"What?" said Imogene, studying the sketch she'd just drawn, trying to decide whether the good shepherd looked sufficiently hirsute.

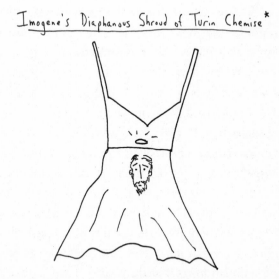

Imogene's Diaphanous Shroud of Turin Chemise[*]

*Despite Patty's insistence that there be no depictions of underclothing in these pages, she eventually relented to the art lovers, voyeurs, illiterates, garment manufacturers, book marketers, and a few UNICEF collectors, all of whom persuaded her to reconsider her position.

33.

Still unsettled by the awards ceremony, Imogene quelled herself to sleep that night by counting the friends of hers for whom a failure, especially one of the heart, might really work wonders.

34.

Meanwhile, Wally got stoned.

35.

Imogene had thirteen voice mails but it was the last one that caught her ear. It was from Ron de Jean. Because of an emergency with the . . . oh, it is too tedious to go into (he says), but anyway, it would be easier (easier for him, she thought, but he does not say this) if they met at the theater instead of beforehand for a bite at Cherry Hill Fats.

The night that Ron de Jean was referring to was the Sunday night Imogene had plans to get together with Wally Yez. Imogene, it appears, had inadvertently double-booked. Again.

(People talk. Behind your back. "What does she see in him?" they say when a twosome walks by. Or else they say, "What does he see in her?" Did Imogene want to play the part of the philanthropist or the charity?)

36.

"Of course I'm disappointed," said Ron when Imogene called him back. He was in fact delighted to have the night off. "But your mother has only two eyes," he said, "so if she's having surgery, then that's that."

"On both eyes," hastened Imogene in case Ron was about to make some kind of spare-eye argument. Imogene felt only slightly bad that she had made up such a thing. Mrs. Gilfeather had never met Ron de Jean, but she probably wouldn't think he was much of a bet and surely wouldn't mind a good lie for a good cause.

Imogene made a point of insisting that she and Ron go out another time soon and Ron was A-OK with that idea. A rule of life, you may have observed, is that pretty much everyone wants to go out, just not right away.

"Can I call you later?" Imogene said because right then her hair needed immediate attention. That idea, too, was A-OK with Ron. The marmalade in his sandwich, he said, was about to leak out and get on his fingers. Not only that, he had to pick his wife up at the airport.

37.

Another rule of life is that everyone wants to get off the phone.

38.

Imogene's mother, Erna Gilfeather, in town for her forti-eth college reunion, has two fine eyes, and she was using them to scrutinize her daughter as they were having afternoon tea at the Plaza. "Honey," she said, whisking a crumb off Imogene's blouse, "are you still making underpants?"

"Lingerie," said Imogene, idly sculpting the butter on her plate with a knife.

"Did I tell you that Norma—remember my college roommate?—her daughter is very high up in human rights?" said Mrs. Gilfeather. Imogene nodded. "So, Immolah, if you want a job doing something of value to society . . ."

"Mother," said Imogene with sullen exasperation. "Featherware is what I do."

Mrs. Gilfeather seemed lost in thought. After a while she said, "Actually, I prefer you when you're gaunt."

39.

When Imogene was in kindergarten, she told the teacher she could not take part in Show and Share because her mother was tired. A short time later, little Imogene was dispatched to talk to the school psychologist, who gave her puzzles and let her sit in any chair. "Imsy," he said, "are you afraid your mother is going to die?" That was the first Imogene had ever heard mention of a mommy dying. The psychologist looked expectantly at Imogene, who shrugged. The psychologist marched Imogene back to her classroom and announced that Imogene never had to take part in Show and Share again. The next week, Imogene was excused from naptime when she said her mother had a bunion. That summer, Imogene was permitted to skip the Nature Walk at day camp after she claimed that her mother had broken hair syndrome.

Despite what Imogene may say, her mother is a healthy old soul. Imogene's father? He is acutely unhealthy. He is dead.

A Word About Imogene's Hair

"My hair is my child," Imogene said on more than one occasion. What did she mean? Let's take a look: Money spent (cumulatively) on crème rinse = tuition to an elite junior college or fairly decent state school plus hefty book allowance. Additional money spent (cumulatively) on cuts and coloring, not to mention round contouring brushes, hair dryers, flatirons, deep-conditioning treatments, detangling serums, styling mousse, sculpting gel, thermal protector, texture spray, damage-control lotion, pH fixer, finishing gloss, barrettes, those elasticky things and miscellaneous items = a four-year Ivy, one year of postgrad, and maybe even a wedding. Also to be considered was the quality time Imogene had spent over the years with her tresses.

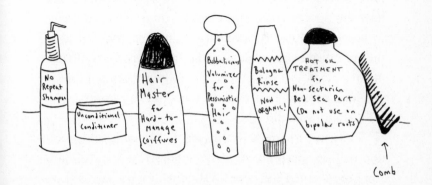

40.

Wouldn't you know it? Imogene had not double-booked, after all. No. She had, in fact, triple-booked the Sunday night she was supposed to go out with Wally Yez. Chronologically speaking, the dinner invitation from the Sepkowitzes, old college buddies of Imogene's, had the edge. "I'm not normally such a blunderhead about these things, truly I'm not," Imogene said as contritely as she could, thinking that would get her off the hook with Wally.

"I love parties. What time?" said Wally, putting her right back on the hook and causing Imogene to wonder: Did she really want to go to a party with someone who loved parties?

41.

Wally was talking to the doorman in Imogene's building, waiting for it to be the minute he'd told Imogene he would be arriving. Wally and the doorman chatted about the agony of the renovation in 3G, the ecstasy of polyurethane foam insulation, the pros and cons of parfait floors (that's how the doorman put it, so, what, you don't want Wally to be polite?), can benevolent dictatorships be so bad if they're called benevolent, why they always make the mates of shoes look like each other, the folly of having a fork if you have a spoon, how to clean a mop, HVAC contractors, BTUs, and, well, life.

So as not to appear overeager, Wally rang Imogene's doorbell 162 seconds after the appointed second. When Imogene opened the door, Wally thrust a package at her. "Just a little something," he said. The package was wrapped in handmade mulberry paper from Thailand and topped with one of Wally's origami paramecia. Wally was particularly proud of the way he had folded the gullet and the feeding groove, but he decided not to mention that. What if Imogene should consider it bragging?

While Imogene daintily unwrapped the package, setting aside the paramecium, presumably for saving purposes, Wally surveyed the apartment and liked what he saw. On a side table sat a pineapple made from crinkled potato chip bags. As soon as Wally saw that pineapple, he thought: Stop the presses! That's it! Imogene Gilfeather, she is the one! He also thought: Nevertheless, why cancel my date for tomorrow night with what's-her-name?

42.

A gift that looks this good on the outside must really be something special inside, or so reasoned Imogene as she, yes, set aside the paramecium for saving purposes. Featherware, in her opinion, was in need of a neat new design for its shopping bags and boxes, and Imogene wondered if bacteria, or whatever a paramecium was, might not prove a market-savvy motif. Imogene removed the lid and came upon a cloud of lime-colored tissue and iridescent crystal fibers. Beneath the fluff was . . . Imogene's hopes were sky-high . . . a rock. To be fair, it was a splendid rock, a rock with glittery strands of turquoise, gold, emerald green, and magenta. And it was of a decent size—not one of those measly chips. Moreover, when Wally presented the gift to Imogene, he *had* said—make no mistake of it—that it was "a little something." Egzzactly.

"It's rainbow hematite from Brazil!" said Wally, snatching the thing out of the box to show Imogene. "They have it all over the place on Mars—not foliated specular hematite like this, but iron ore, which, of course, is what gives the planet its rusty red color." Wally handed the rock to Imogene. "Hematite has a relatively high specific gravity," he said, "but I don't think that will be a problem for you." Wally laughed. Was this at all humorous? Imogene decided—what the heck—to laugh, anyway.

"It's very nice," said Imogene, though between you and me, she felt a little disappointed and also felt a lot guilty about her disappointment, knowing as well as anyone: it's supposed to be the thought that counts.

"I was going to get you zincobotryogen," said Wally, "but I didn't think you and I had come to a point where we were ready for that."

43.

The reader will appreciate that Imogene, unlike Wally, was neither an animal nor a mineral person. Imogene was a vegetable person.

44.

Besides Wally and Imogene, here's who was at the Sepkowitzes' that night: a photographer who just had a show at the Whitney Museum (nudes), a photographer dying to have a show at the Whitney Museum (old people wearing clothes), a journalist writing a piece for a journalism

review about journalism (brought a bag of "authentic gla-
cier water" ice cubes to the dinner), a woman who quit her
high-rolling corporate lawyer job to become a teacher in
the slums, a man who quit his teaching job in the slums to
go to law school, a lawyer-turned-senator currently working on a bill to make wagons, toboggans, and other means of
alternative transportation tax-deductible, a clothes designer
from Bhutan who'd just been hired to create a new look
for the Rockettes, a woman poet writing a novel about a
woman writing a poem-within-a-poem, a man who said
he did nothing but think all day, a man who was studying the evolution of disgust, the producer of the hit sketch
comedy television show *Taped but Proud,* and his wife, a
shoe designer intent on making the "retractable high heel"
a household word, a woman who wrote a syndicated golf
column in which she interviewed notable golfers and cut
them down to size, a woman who said she believed in Santa
Claus until she was fourteen, a married couple who'd written the definitive cookbook about organ meats, a man who
claimed he came up with the idea of putting fruit in yogurt
(but unfortunately never patented it), and, of course, the
Sepkowitzes, who were both accountants.

Meg Sepkowitz telephoned Imogene the next day.
"Richard and I really like Wally," said Meg, "and we were
wondering: How are you going to fuck it up?"

45.

"I have my ways," thought Imogene.

46.

That day in Wallyland, Wally and Derek were trying to build a rack for Derek's atomic clock. (For those readers who bought the discount version of this book that does not include the Who's Who or the letter Q, Derek is Wally's best friend.)

"See anything?" Wally's friend Derek said, putting on a pair of safety goggles.

"I wasn't looking. I was thinking," Wally said.

"You were out with a professional underwear specialist," said Derek. "And didn't sneak a peek?"

"No, but I still had maybe, let's see, the fifth-best time of my life," said Wally.

Derek fired up the oxyacetylene torch. "You know what the only thing she said to me at the party was?" Wally said, but Derek couldn't hear. "She said, 'I think I'm going to leave now, but you should feel free to stay.'" Was Derek muttering something to himself? Wally thought he might be, but it was hard to know. Derek turned off the torch and adjusted his goggles.

"I'm not a complete troglodyte," Wally said. "Of course, I didn't let her leave alone, but outside, when I asked her if she wanted to have a drink, she said she had work to do and wanted to go home."

47.

"What was the third-best time?" Derek said.

48.

"To tell you the truth, the entire night, I don't think I made eye contact with the guy once," said Imogene to her assistant. They were packing up boxes of sample panty hose to send to the National Hosiery Convention in Houston.

"What does he do?" said Harriet, rummaging through a carton. "Fishnets with or without a seam?"

"What does who do?" said Imogene. "Forget the fishnets. Fishnets are not Houston. Fishnets are maybe Dallas."

"Willy or Walter or whatever," said Harriet.

"How do I know?" said Imogene. "It's too awkward to talk to a stranger at a party. Or, for that matter, anywhere." Imogene sealed up a carton of dove-gray sheers and slate-gray ultrasheers, fastidiously applying the packing tape, even though straight lines would not matter to anyone but herself. "He seemed to spend a lot of time doing magic tricks for the Sepkowitz twins," Imogene said. She worried: Could Wally be a magician?

"I love magic," said Harriet.

"Too much abracadabra," said Imogene, placing a stack of steel-gray control tops in a carton. "Cross your fingers, but I really think the Saks thing will happen."

"Wow," said Harriet.

"Let's put it this way," Imogene said. "I spent the better part of the party on the phone with the buyer, who said they definitely have a hole in their mid-range lingerie department."

"Do you think the guy will call again?" said Harriet.

"Donald Charm? He all but promised," said Imogene.

"No," said Harriet. "Not the Saks guy. The other guy. He sounds dreamy—and such fun."

"Fun," said Imogene, "is not fun." She held up a pair of synthetic leather leggings that resembled eggplant skin and furrowed her brow. "What do you think, is Texas a faux state or not?"

49.

Would Wally call again? Wasn't Imogene even a smidgen curious? Of course, to question one. And the other question? To quote Imogene: "No."

50.

Wally and Imogene made a second date.

51.

Again, Imogene had something else to do the night in question, except this time the "something else" was arranged afterward. Ron de Jean had invited her to the third game of the World Series and, though Imogene had limited interest in baseball, a hard-to-get ticket is a hard-to-get ticket. The hard-to-get ticket had become gettable when Ron's wife, theoretically the world's leading expert on Little Red Riding Hood, had to leave town unexpectedly for France after a colleague called with the news that there'd been a discovery about the Wolf in the Dordogne.

52.

There's a connection, if you have not already figured it out, between Ron's wife's being away and Imogene's being with Ron.

53.

Look for further evidence in twenty-five pages.

54.

On second thought, these things can be hard for Patty to keep track of. Would it be so terrible if we said *give or take* twenty-five pages? On third thought: forget the first thought.

55.

On fourth thought: about her affair with Ron, Imogene said, "It never ends, and it never starts." This is the way Imogene felt about her life, too. She had no complaints with either.

56.

Imogene canceled Date #2.

"Boating accident," said Imogene to Wally on the telephone because *The Old Man and the Sea* was on TV and she couldn't think of anything else. Wally seemed very understanding, which made Imogene suffer all the more insufferably. He offered to drive her down to New Jersey to be with her mother in the hospital.

Out of guilt and perhaps another feeling, too, she suggested they make a plan then and there. "But this time, let's wood-burn the date into our calendars," she said, as if Wally had been the culprit in mucking up the schedule twice before. Then—she couldn't help herself—she added gravely, "Assuming there aren't, you know, complications."

57.

That night, Imogene's mother called, as she did most Sundays. And Tuesdays. And the rest of the week. Imogene was in the midst of rearranging the furniture in her living room. "Darling," Erna Gilfeather said, "you still haven't told me whether you're coming home for Thanksgiving."

"That's one, two, three . . ."—she counted on her fingers—"five months from now," said Imogene. "I just started shipping swimwear." Imogene shoved the wing chair so that it was perpendicular to the coffee table. Don't go overboard with diagonals, her mother had taught her long ago.

"If you do come home, are you bringing anyone?" said Mrs. Gilfeather. "I need to know what size turkey to order."

Maybe the coffee table needed to be over there, thought Imogene. If only she could move the fireplace a little that way, too.

"Bring someone," said Erna Gilfeather. "It'll make the dinner tolerable."

58.

Does Wally have a mother?

59.

Everyone has a mother.

60.

It's one of those things. Like soil erosion.

61.

Yes, the chaplettes are brief. The intention had been panoramic longness but, apparently, everything cannot be under anybody's control. Even Patty's.

62.

In the days since Imogene had canceled their date, Wally had been feeling low. How low? -1.04. Is that not low enough for you? Tonight was to have been *the* night. Instead, it was another night. Wally was skimming through a recent issue of *Reptiles Plus Monthly,* intrigued by a squib about how to tell if your turtle is fat, when he came across the results of the prestigious Southern States Tortoise Contest in Boca Raton. Wally could not believe his eyes! Without telling him, Gwen had entered Stuffy, their Mediterranean spur-thighed tortoise (*Testudo graeca*), in the competition. The creature had won an orange ribbon, placing First Runner-Up. It was true that Wally had begrudgingly given Gwen custody of Stuffy when Wally and Gwen had split up. But turning Stuffy into a professional without first asking Wally's opinion about the matter . . . why, it is not done! To treat a man and a turtle like that! How dare she?

Wally turned on the television, with the hope that he might see Imogene. The chances of that happening were slim—Wally realized that. He was no fool. But Wally was big on slim chances. "One hundred percent of big lottery winners had infinitesimally small odds of becoming lottery winners" was one of the truisms Wally lived his life by.

Today, however, Wally was not a lottery winner. Imogene was not to be seen on the shopping channel, hawking Featherware; she was not on the cooking channel, whipping up soufflés (or was it éclairs?); she was not on the local news, being interviewed about the polite neighbor who kept to himself except when he was chopping up the family next door; she was not on *The Sit on the Sofa with Penny Jackson Show,* chit-chatting with Penny; she was not on the reality show *Hey, You: Wanna Land a Plane?*

Oh, the places Imogene was not! They could fill a book. Not this book. An atlas.

63.

Wally picked up the phone and called Imogene, whose number he had, by then, unfortunately memorized.

64.

When Wally called Imogene, a recorded message coldly informed him that she was unavailable. This caused Wally to miss Gwen more than a little on account of her availability. Wally tried Imogene's number again.

And reached her.

65.

Regarding chaplette 62: Patty would like it known that she was highly impressed with herself for spelling the word *infinitesimally* correctly on the second try.

66.

Wally's neck did not need shaving, but it was Friday night and he really had nothing else to do. "What did you two talk about until three in the morning?" said Elsie.

Elsie also had nothing to do. Apparently, lots of people did have things to do, because Wally was the only customer in the salon that night. Again, Elsie ran the clippers over a fallow patch on Wally's neck because she wanted to give Wally his money's worth and, as has been stated, she and Wally really had nothing else to do.

"Until three-twenty," said Wally. "I guess we talked mostly about how perfect she thought her life was and how overrated she thought relationships were and how I disagreed. We talked a little about curved ferrite rods, too."

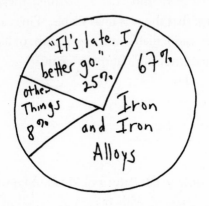

What Wally and Imogene Talked About

67.

Imogene's calendar was booked for the next decade. What Imogene wanted more than anything was time.

68.

Correction: what Imogene wanted more than anything was for Donald Charm, the Saks buyer, to say yes tomorrow at lunch.

69.

Pockets of drizzle in Iowa led to airport delays in Chicago, which led to lost luggage up and down the Eastern Seaboard, which led to Donald Charm's canceling the lunch with Imogene. Imogene and Wally sat in the park that day eating hot dogs from the hot dog man.

"Can I ask you something?" said Imogene. "Why do you have all those condiments?"

"I've been disappointed a lot in my life," said Wally. He paused. "You're not condimephobic, are you?"

70.

Though he knew full well that nobody desires the desirous, Wally e-mailed Imogene the moment he returned home from the park. He wanted, needed, to tell Imogene that, according to his numbers, the two of them had so far accrued only $^{107}/_{120}$ of a proper date together, calculated thus:

1. Sepkowitzes' party (223 words exchanged; approximately 7 seconds of physical contact between them) = $^{1}/_{6}$ of a date.

2. Accumulated phone calls (4 hours, 10 minutes' duration; both parties talking from bed, under covers) = $\frac{1}{8}$ of a date.
3. Lunch (outdoors; no alcohol; plastic utensils) = $\frac{3}{5}$ of a date.

Total Amount of Date = $\frac{107}{120}$

This news came plangently to Imogene, as plangently as any news had ever come plangently to her. Imogene, you see, had been under the impression, to the extent Imogene had any impression at all, that she and Wally had racked up two official dates.

71.

Two out of a possible two.

72.

What Wally wanted more than anything was love.

73.

Ahhh.

74·

On a whim or worse, Imogene *handwrote* a note to Wally. As soon as she dropped it in the mailbox, she wished she had not. What kind of a person sends a thank-you for a hot dog? Would Wally even remember the hot dog? Wasn't it braggy of her to mention Saks in the second paragraph? That reference to the Rise and Fall of Roman Polanski? What was that about? Why did she write *whom* instead of *who* in that sentence? Why had she written that sentence, anyway? What about the cute postscript? Oh God, the stupid post-postscript! Why had she included her other telephone number? Did she really invite him to . . . she couldn't even think about that. How about the stationery? It was the same stationery she used for condolences. Nobody uses stationery anymore. Not even for dead people. Why oh why oh why oh why had she signed off, "Hugs and kisses"?

75·

That's not who she was.

76.

Was it?

77.

Imogene clenched her hands and closed her eyes. "I don't even like him," she thought. "He's too enthusiastic about things I don't care about and his sweater was inside-out." She remembered the moons on his thumbnails. She didn't like those either.

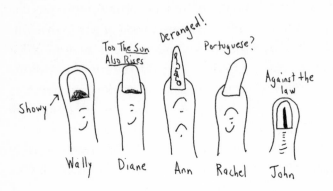

78.

When Wally's friend Derek phoned, Wally was idly watching a bar of soap pucker and bubble and then expand monstrously in the microwave.

"Hey," said Derek, "want to meet this gal who's, like, twenty-three and drop-dead cute?"

"I'm in the middle of something crucial," said Wally, replacing the glop on the carousel cooking tray with a hundred-watt lightbulb. "Twenty seconds should do it," he thought.

"Aw, come on," said Derek. "Normally, you'd have to be a runty billionaire to get near someone with those credentials."

"What's the catch?" said Wally. The lightbulb pulsated with emanations of color, and then popped, shattering into smithereens. "You're single last time I checked."

"Me? With her?" said Derek. "My mother would murder me." Beenish Asif, explained Derek, was his second cousin. She'd just arrived in New York from Saskatchewan, having exhausted the natural male resources of Canada. Derek had promised his aunt and stepuncle he'd take care of their daughter in the city, where she was getting her masters in Applied Sex Education. "Besides," said Derek. "Don't you need someone to take your mind off what's-her-name?"

"Imogene," said Wally. The steel wool pad being zapped at the highest frequency emitted a shower of sparkle.

Now you know how Wally came to spend the night with Beenish Asif.

79.

Wally met Beenish Asif downtown at a bar of her choosing—a hole in the wall called Fire Hazard even though smoking was prohibited. "How will I recognize you?" Wally had asked on the phone. Beenish could have said she had an overbite, a China doll haircut, and a tiny scar under her left eyebrow from an EZ-Bake Oven accident (it was all true), but she didn't. Instead, she said, "My contact lenses are tinted green."

"Anything else?" said Wally.

"I'm kind of dyslexic, I love teriyaki, and I had my adenoids removed last year," she said.

Was Beenish being alluringly goofy or was she not so

bright? Patty has thought about this, and wants to keep her hands clean. Wally, beguiled by the fizziness of Beenish's voice as well as her availability, is not a reliable judge, ever. He was pathologically generous.

"One more thing," said Beenish before she and Wally hung up. "When I go to a movie, I like to sit in the front row."

80.

What Beenish Asif wanted more than anything was a good time, especially if it involved taking her clothes off and/or food.

81.

Because Fire Hazard was so crowded that only a pickpocket could be happy there, Wally and Beenish retired down the block to her sublet. Besides, Beenish had to feed her cat. Beenish did not, in fact, care for cats, and the feeling was mutual. Why did she have a cat? Because: Who has time to walk a dog?

As anyone who has read chaplette 24 knows, Wally's job was more or less to kill cats in the name of Science. When Wally met Beenish's cat, he knelt down and stroked the patch of fur under its chin.

82.

Let's give Wally credit.

83.

He appears to know the difference between work and play.

84.

"I think I figured it out," Derek said to Wally, who was loosening an obstreperous screw. They were in Derek's basement, trying to modify a radio scanner so they could decrypt digital cellular phone conversations. Derek continued. "You'd be my third cousin, or is it my second cousin once removed?"

"For the millionth time," said Wally, "I'm not marrying Beenish." He took something off of something.

"Is it because you don't want to sit next to me at family gatherings, cuz?" said Derek with pseudo-concern as he patted Wally's shoulder in a mock-avuncular way. (The shoulder, however, was real.)

"Cut it out," said Wally. "You know I'm in love with Imogene." He held out his palm in expectation. "Long-nose pliers."

Derek handed Wally the tool kit. "How do you know Imogene's in love with you?"

"Didn't she invite me to see an exhibit about textiles from ancient Egypt?" said Wally, who scrunched up his face as he tightened the tricky connector that stuck out from the back of the scanner.

"And didn't she disinvite you in that P.P.S.?" Derek said.

"She sent me a thank-you note for a hot dog," said Wally. "Who sends someone a thank-you note for a hot dog?"

"Maybe a hot dog nut," said Derek.

"No, I feel unique," Wally and Derek heard a scratchy voice on the radio say. They breathed not a breath to make sure that what they heard wasn't merely a scratch. "Everyone here is a Mormon," the scratchy voice said, "but I am the only *dormant* Mormon."

85.

Wally e-mailed Imogene, thanking her for thanking him for the hot dog. "Did you know that this year Americans will eat enough hot dogs at major league ballparks to stretch from RFK Stadium in Washington, D.C., to AT&T Park in San Francisco?" was the last sentence in his brief e-mail. On the next line there was a *W* (no period after it).

Imogene replied that she had not even known that there was an AT&T Park in San Francisco. She signed her e-mail "I" (no period at the end). It looked a lot like the number 1, she thought, but such was the story of her life. She put a period at the end, then took it away, then put it back. She went back and forth, adding and deleting a dot, which was probably of concern to only Imogene. (Not even Patty cares a fig.) This, as well, was the story of her life. Finally, she went with the period, deciding that otherwise the poor *I* looked stranded. But this, she felt certain, was not the story of her life.

86.

Thus began the e-mail correspondence of Wally Yez and Imogene Gilfeather.

87.

At first, they e-mailed in moderation, usually at night and mostly recounting the whatever and whatnot of the day.

88.

"Watched a documentary about how they make Pyrex measuring cups."

89.

"Got a scratch on my new eyeglasses."

90.

"Did you get caught in that downpour?"

91.

"The thing was so rusty it took two hours to take off seven screws."

92.

"Still recovering from that expedition to the post office."

93.

"I must tell you about my new bathroom mat."

94.

"Only if I can tell you about my refrigerator condenser."

95.

"Guess how much my shoe guy charges to put rubber taps on a pair of boots?"

96.

Four and a half more shopping days until chaplette 100.

97.

The e-mails became longer. Wally told Imogene about his outing to Brooklyn, where he toured a mechanical room containing the oldest running steam-powered direct current generator still in operation. He did not tell her about the dynamos and boilers he saw in action, because he wanted to surprise her with those stories the next time they were together. Imogene told Wally about the dinner party she'd gone to where an audio loop of a party that sounded more rollicking was playing in the background. Imogene omitted the detail that she was the hostess of the party. Nor did she include the fact that among the guests was Ron de Jean.

98.

"I can promise you neither time nor devotion," Imogene wrote in an e-mail.

"I'll settle for one or the other," Wally e-mailed back. "You pick."

99.

Imogene did not answer.

99½.

Despite that lapse, their e-mailing picked up its pace. Once a day became two times a day became on the hour became continual became unbearable. Fifty-two pages of pillow talk. Same as a deck of cards, observed Wally, who, as a master of close-up magic, did not take the coincidence lightly.

100.

Merry Centasection! To recap: 53 pages, 99½ chaplettes, 371 paragraphs, 53,056 characters (with no spaces), 53,017 characters (with spaces). Patty thinks she is strongest in chaplettes and paragraphs. And character.

So many characters. Yes, it's hard to keep them straight, especially the *S*'s. Ha ha.

101.

Business (or, as Patty prefers to call it, art) as usual hereby resumes.

102.

"How would you like to take part in a bold experiment?" Wally e-mailed Imogene a few weeks into their cyberfest.

103.

Imogene, while no fan of the scientific method, agreed, despite some qualms, to go along with the bold experiment. Rather than exchange e-mails, she and Wally would venture into actual conversation—not in person, for that would be *too* bold, but phonewise. Yes, they'd spoken before, but they barely knew each other. It was easier to fabricate data then.

104.

That night, Wally called Imogene at eleven o'clock on the dot.

105.

Science is precise.

106.

"Mr. Watson—come here—I want to see you," began Wally. He told Imogene that those words were the first that Alexander Graham Bell uttered over the telephone. Then he gave Imogene a lecture about how a telephone works.

107.

Science can explain so much.

108.

And what a number 108 is. Brings back memories.

109.

Plus, it's the atomic number of hassium, you jerk.

110.

Soon Wally and Imogene were talking on the phone every eleven o'clock on the dot until every three or four in the morning. After a few weeks, however, Imogene informed Wally that at this point in her career it was now or never and she happened to prefer now, which meant, romantically speaking, that she did not have the time to be, as she put it, "embroiled."

Earlier that day—it was not a coincidence—Imogene had learned that a competitor of Featherware, a company called Blatant Exploitation, had just sold its First Amendment Briefs ("Endorsed by the ACLU!") to Saks Fifth Avenue.

"I'm not saying your career's not important," Wally told her. "But I think it's also now or never for you to build a history with someone." Wally adjusted his pillows and turned off the light on his night table. "Have you, I'm wondering, ever factored in the cumulative effect of checking in with a person, the same person, every night in bed?"

111.

First science, now history.

112.

"What is this," thought Imogene, "school?"

113.

Being a diligent student, Imogene tried her best to picture a union such as the one Wally extolled. What would it feel like, she mused, to share a scrapbook of memories with somebody? To have an index of proper nouns in common with this somebody so that nobody had to explain, for instance, who Bruce Strober was? To know someone's memories so deeply she would sometimes wonder, hey, did that happen to him or to me? To talk in a secret shorthand nobody else understood—and even, when they felt like it, not to talk at all? To have cutesy pet names? What would it be like to be so assured about another that she went around the house in sweatpants, wearing no makeup—well, maybe a touch of blush—and, then, as Wally said, to check in with each other that night no matter what?

114.

Awful, she thought.

115.

Really terrible. P.U.

116.

When the night became too long, she imagined her funeral. Who would be in attendance might have been entrancing enough speculation for others, but not for Imogene. She wondered whose funerals, among her mourners, she would skip, should death arrive in a different order.

117.

The next night, while she was in bed, her speakerphone on, Imogene heard an exposition from Wally about flight distance, the term used by animal behaviorists to describe how close one can get to an animal critter before the animal takes off. So as not to seem like too much of a weirdo and in the interest of being polite, Imogene rounded down and told Wally that she guessed her FD was about twelve city blocks. Wally told Imogene that the conjoined twin model was more apt to describe him.

"Which reminds me," said Wally, "where would you like to spend your old age? In the country for me."

"Definitely the city," said Imogene.

"I wish you would stop going out of your way to point out how different we are," said Wally.

"Good night," said Imogene.

"Good night," said Wally.

118.

Was that a fight?

119.

What is going on here?

120.

Hard to know. Dark clouds overhead? Cream curdling? Hard drive crashing?

121.

The next night, Imogene did not pick up the phone at the appointed hour. Wally thought he'd dialed wrong and dialed back. He started to dial again, but put the telephone down, figuring Imogene was brushing her teeth. The last thing Wally wanted to do was encourage Imogene to interrupt herself in mid-brush. He tried later. He had it in mind to tell her about his cousin who'd chipped his tooth in the process of trying to bite open the stuck toothpaste cap. He would warn Imogene not to do this. But there was still no answer. And none still later. Wally began to worry. He imagined that debris from scaffolding had fallen on top of her; that she had plunged to her death in an elevator; been crushed by falling bookshelves; poisoned by sushi meant for a diplomat; shot by a cannon during a performance of *Aida*; fatally attached to a superstrong magnet; attacked by a horse that resented having to drag tourists in carriages through the streets of the city when even a horse can see they could have taken the bus.

122.

What never occurred to Wally was that Imogene was spending the night with Ron de Jean.

123.

Wally perused the owner's manual that came with his camera. Ordinarily, nothing gave Wally more pleasure than a thick instruction booklet. "It's always the same when I turn that last page," Wally was known to say, "I just can't hold back the flat-out catharsis and exhilaration." Tonight, however, all the tips in the world about installation, operation, and troubleshooting could not boost Wally's spirits.

124.

Wally called Derek to report that the worst had befallen the love of his life.

125.

"Need your brother to issue ABT for a 507," Wally texted Elsie, his longstanding barber, de facto therapist, and tight familial link to the New York Police Department. Wally meant an APB (all-points bulletin) for a 10-57 (missing person). What he'd written had something to do with the American Ballet Theater and a public nuisance.

"HA HA," Elsie texted back. "CM IN IMMED 4 EMERGCY SHAMPOO."

126.

Wally was so overwrought that he decided to calm himself down by making a list of batteries: polymer battery (of course), biobattery, nuclear microbattery, optoelectric nuclear battery, organic radical battery, Baghdad battery, nanobattery, paper battery, supercharged ion, nickel cadmium, 9-volt, dry cell, button battery, AAAA, lithium, lantern battery, AAA, C, D, AA, lemon battery.

There are many other types of batteries, but this was as far as Wally got before his sleeping pill kicked in.

127.

The next night, Wally distracted himself by going with Beenish Asif to the opening of the Pakistani Film Festival. A tweet by one of her classmates about a little-known Indian massacre of thirty-five Pakistanis in an upscale Lahore suburb had been made into a movie.

128.

A comedy. (Not a bad one.)

129.

After the film, there was a party with plenty of Pakistani bigwigs but no booze. After the party, Beenish and Wally went to Beenish's, where there was Courvoisier V.S.O.P. While Beenish was in the bathroom, Wally made a beeline to the kitchen to make a quick call to you-know-who.

He let the phone ring six times and would have let it ring until infinity if Beenish had not shown up in the kitchen, mascara-tinged tears running down her cheeks. Beenish was crying, she said, because her signature perfume (Gunsmoke) was being discontinued, because she was allergic to her favorite nut (macadamia), because, as she'd heard on the radio, the senator from Vermont was still filibustering and he sounded tired, because there was a full moon out, because she was not alone tonight (tears of joy), and because Beenish was a world-class crier.

Wally followed Beenish into the bedroom because Imogene sure wasn't waiting for him.

(A 65 percent chance of a mix of clouds and sun was in the forecast. What the other 35 percent might be up to, nobody said.)

130.

This time Imogene really was brushing her teeth. Then she stayed up late, occupied with a million things. She looked through catalogs, scrubbed the wall moldings and inspected the cornices, drank two espressos, turned the television on while she paid her utility bill and then off while she treated herself to a normalizing facial mask, and telephoned Harriet to discuss the ins and outs of inventory. Imogene surmised that Wally had dozed off before the appointed hour.

131.

Where was Imogene the night before chaplette 129?

132.

She was, as has been noted, with Ron de Jean. Ron de Jean's wife had e-mailed Ron de Jean to say, "Do not come to collect me at the airport, I will not be on Flight 343 on account of a development at the Hood conference having to do with the Woodsman."

133.

Ron was not sure whether she meant this as a single or double entendre.

134.

Ron de Jean had little time to be perplexed. His lab assistant had informed him that one of the subjects in the sleep experiment was still sleeping. Every now and again, big anxiety gets in the way of little anxiety.

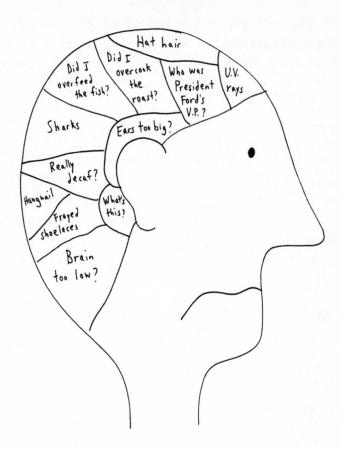

135.

Or is it the other way around?

136.

"As in sleeping or as in *sleeping*?" Ron said with suppressed terror in his voice.

"The good news is that the molecule is indeed sopo-rific," said the assistant.

Oh, well, Science!

137.

Ron called Imogene from the hospital. "If there's any-thing I can do—" she said, meaning, of course, please don't ask me to do anything. Wasn't just offering enough? Not according to Ron, alas. He did not want to be alone that night, he said.

138.

Imogene did.

139.

Ron won.

140.

The subject woke up, if you could call it that.

141.

But enough about the subject. Let's go back to the lab, shall we?

142.

No. The other lab.

143.

The vestibulospinal reflex lab. It was there that Wally and Gwen used to work side by side, rolling, pitching, and yawing cats around until the felines were unable to keep up appearances. More recently, it was there near the elevator that Wally bumped into his former partner.

144.

He was getting in, Gwen was getting out.

145.

The large, flimsy-looking carton in Wally's arms concealed his face from her, but Gwen recognized the sneakers (black leather, blue suede), which she had purchased ($124.38) the day before Wally left her (four months, eleven days ago).

146.

Gwen stepped back into the elevator. "What a surprise to see you," she said, even though she sort of couldn't see him. "Maybe we should have a cup of coffee and, you know, talk." Gwen pressed the button for the ground floor.

147.

"Don't tell me you're pregnant again," thought Wally. Anyway, hadn't Gwen walked out on him a long time ago (at least seven months)? Wally had all the womenfolk he could handle right now (one to four, depending on how he counted). "I've already had too many cups of coffee," he said. (Three and a half.)

148.

The elevator came to a stop and the carton broke, its contents spilling all over. "Why are you taking your stapler home?" asked Gwen, surprised again.

149.

Wally thought, "She doesn't want my stapler, does she?"

150.

Over a cup of tea, Wally told Gwen that he had just resigned from the lab.

"Because of me?" she said.

"No," he said, and for a moment, he forgot who she was.

151.

Gwen was curious if the waitress was one of the things Wally wanted to pursue.

152.

"Tell me the truth," Gwen said. "Did you leave because I went down to Insect Neuro?"

"I left because I developed an unscientific attachment to cats," said Wally.

"So what will you kill now?" said Gwen.

"I'll guess I'll come up with something," Wally said.

Gwen nibbled her rice snack in silence. She licked her finger, and with it gathered the last of the crumbs. "I think I should have joint custody of the car," she said.

(Gwen was not pregnant, but she was back with Leonard from the lab.)

153.

Some would say that among their rendezvous thus far, Wally and Imogene's stroll through the park was the most auspicious. It was the first summery day of spring so the lawns were scattered with stripped-down sunbathers whose winter flesh Patty chooses not to describe.

"Are you seeing anyone else?" Wally asked Imogene, taking her hand under the pretense he was helping her over a stick. "Because I don't want to fall for you if you are with somebody else." Wally did not tell Imogene that it was too late, that he had already fallen. Instead, he told her that he did not feel he could take another big step with her right now because he was too worried about being made heavy-hearted. If things didn't work out, that is.

"I understand," said Imogene, but of course, she did not understand. She said it was okay with her if they stopped now. And she meant it. Then nothing happened, except Wally almost got walloped by a bicyclist.

154.

When nothing happens:
   a) You still have to pay.
   b) Count your lucky stars.
   c) Replace the battery.
   d) Something is happening, but very, very slowly.

155.

The severity of the phenomenon in the region may be attributed to the collision of two barometric pressures over a body of water. Heat index high. Wind chill factor low.

The above took place atop Imogene's extra-firm mattress. Meteorologists were baffled.

156.

Imogene was not in the habit of talking about her private life or even about her semiprivate life. But as long as Imogene had her mouth open, she figured she might as well use it. She told the dental hygienist quite a bit about the happenings of the night before. During the scaling, polishing, opening wider, and turn a little to me, please, Imogene yackety-yakked.

Then, after the final rinse, the hygienist spoke up.

157.

"What?" the hygienist said.

158.

"What did you say?"

159.

"Were you saying something?"

160.

"I thought I heard you say something."

161.

Wally was getting a haircut. Wally's hair, however, was not the point. "She's the girl," he said to Elsie as Elsie snipped. "She's the one."

"That's what you always say," said Elsie. "They shouldn't let you use that number anymore. They should make you start at maybe seven."

"This time is different," said Wally.

"Stop squirming," said Elsie. "This thing I'm holding is sharp."

"Imogene is the love of my life," said Wally.

"That's what you said about what's-her-name," said Elsie.

"Her?" said Wally. "I never said I was in love with— wait, what was her name?"

162.

Susan.

163.

Wally never knew. Don't give him credit. Patty knew. She has an impeccable memory for the inconsequential.

164.

Let us go back. We'd better hurry up and go back!

165.

Once upon a time, on the outskirts of a hamlet, there dwelt a poor cobbler and his wife.

166.

Not that far back. Let's say only a few hours.

167.

Sure enough, nothing lasts forever—not even nothing. Before long something was happening again. Wally had dropped by Imogene's apartment, claiming he was in the neighborhood, which, by definition, he was. "I'm not doing anything," said Imogene, who'd been darning.

Wally stayed the night, and what a night it was. This,

however, is not one of those books in which the author delineates every disgusting detail. What a pity. If it were one of those books, Patty wouldn't be living in an apartment worse than Imogene's.

168.

Blinking aside, Wally did not close his eyes that night. His full regard focused on Imogene, who seemed to be in sound repose. And yet, the next day, it was Wally who felt refreshed and vigorous and Imogene who was beat. How would Ron de Jean, sleep expert extraordinaire, explain this?

169.

This is not a rhetorical question.

170.

Nonetheless, Patty will not answer it.

171.

The girl who sidled up to Wally the next morning on the subway worked as a wardrobe consultant on photo shoots, specializing in wind, both natural and machine generated, but apparently she knew how to look adorable in the doldrums as well. Wally, however, was too moony-eyed over

Imogene to notice. Wally told the girl all about Imogene. Which seemed to make the girl more interested.

172.

Wally got off at the next stop and never looked back.

173.

Life is unfair.

174.

Here's who else Wally told about Imogene: the woman at the curb waiting for a green light, the newspaper stand fellow, the counter clerk at the dry cleaner, the delivery boy, the guy who telephoned Wally but meant to telephone Wee Lae Fong (one digit away) to order pork dumplings, Derek.

A dog in an elevator.

Wally did not tell the lady squashed next to him on the bus who was reading her Bible as if she were cramming for the afterlife.

175.

"Whatever you do," Imogene said to Wally moments before Erna Gilfeather opened the front door to her raised ranch-style house, "don't tell my mother you've seen me naked."

"What if she tortures me?" said Wally, playfully elbowing Imogene in the ribs.

Imogene stood up straight and brushed a strand of hair off her forehead. "And please don't tell her I lost her garnet earrings," she said. Wally mimed sealing his lips.

"Also, not a word about my forgetting to vote," said Imogene, "or about the jeans she keeps begging me to throw out or that I reuse ziplock bags, keep textile dye in the refrigerator, have consumed alcohol, had a mole biopsied, take the subway at night, never wrote a thank-you note to Aunt Anne, watered her silk plants for a week, or committed copyright violations."

"Let's sleep in your old room," said Wally, exuberantly throwing his arms around his beloved.

"No touching me in front of her," said Imogene, recoiling. "Or looking at me."

The door opened. "Happy Thanksgiving," said Mrs. Gilfeather, kissing her daughter on the earlobe. "How was the traffic, Doug?" Mrs. Gilfeather asked Wally. He thought it best not to correct her.

176.

After warning Wally about how irksome her mother could be, Imogene was disappointed that the visit, exploding turkey aside, had not been a fiasco.

"Your mother's not so bad," said Wally on the drive back to New York.

"Why do you have to be so generous?" thought Imogene.

177.

Hold everything. You, who have so valiantly struggled to follow the story of Wally and Imogene,* which has often been told willy-nilly and heedless of caution, may have forgotten this detail, which we would like to recollect.

The time is one hundred forty-seven chaplettes ago. The place is the First Annual International Silhouette Lingerie Awards. A model was found with the dissociative drug ketamine. On her person.

Users of ketamine have reported conversations with Higher Powers and with halibut. More pertinently, the drug is illegal. More pertinently still, the drug was traced to the very lab from which Wally Yez had just resigned.

Do you know who seems to find this information particularly pertinent? The two police officers who show up at Wally's door.

178.

Sick and tired of insomnia, Imogene turned on the television and caught the predawn local news. Wally did not seem the type, she thought, listening to the crime reporter. But then she thought that it is always the type who does not seem the type who turns out to be the type. Also, wasn't it premature of the local news to name names? Maybe even unconstitutional? Then again, Imogene has a habit of thinking that whatever it is that nonplusses her might

---

*You think you've got problems. It hasn't been easy for Patty to figure this whole thing out either.

be against the Constitution. Which she confuses with the Declaration of Independence. Which she confuses with the Bill of Rights. Don't bring up the Articles of Confederation. Which may or may not be the same as the Federalist Papers.

179.

Imogene is not nonplussed about the word *nonplus*.

180.

One thing Imogene knows: you are innocent until proven guilty. But she also knows that where there's smoke, there's fire. Plus, don't shoot until you see the whites of their eyes. Let's not forget better safe than sorry. *C'est la vie.*

So once again, Imogene did not know (or care). If Imogene were to pick up the telephone right now, she could find out the truth, but there is no comfort in the truth. Here is what you get with truth: the remarks they made about you after you left the room, a rundown of the bacteria on your hotel pillow, the identity of your real father, the hard facts about that shadow missed by the doctor reading the MRI, what you look like from behind.

If Imogene or Wally knew the truth, this little book would come to an abrupt end.

181.

The end. Period.

A CATALOGUE OF PERIODS

Italicized

Disguised as
a dot

Disguised as
a comma

In love

Drunk!

... Stuttering

Nerdy

Used by
Thomas Jefferson

Full of itself

Medieval

Art Deco

Art Noveau

Stealthy

Dormant

182.

No, no, no. It is just that ever since this project began, Patty has been weighted down by a foreboding sense that sooner or later the end must come. But now, with the anticipation of those words behind us, we can continue with composure. For there is plenty more to tell.

Oh. One more thing has been a burden for Patty, if she may please interrupt again. Ever since chaplette 168, she has been worried that crucial facts have been forgotten or started to fade. So, herewith, is the recap.

183.

Imogene Gilfeather. Featherware Lingerie. Saks Fifth Avenue. Wally Yez. Trouble with Gwen. Ron de Jean. Married. Wally woos Imogene. Imogene busy. Assistant is Harriet. Inventory to pack. Undergarments to sell. Hair to dry (Imogene's). Wally more in love. Elsie, hairdresser, heard it before. Stuffy, ex-tortoise, wins prize. (Go, Stuffy!) Imogene's mother quote unquote sick again. Derek says, "Wally, meet Beenish Asif." Beenish Asif and Wally have Courvoisier V.S.O.P. Wally and Imogene have hot dog. Wally and Imogene e-mail. They talk. Patty spells *infinitesimally.* Wally sleeps at Beenish Asif's. Trouble in Ron de Jean's sleep lab. Ron sleeps at Imogene's. Gwen sleeps with Leonard. Is Ron de Jean's wife sleeping with "Woodsman"? Wally sleeps at Imogene's. Imogene tells Wally, "Nobody but you." Wally does not sleep. Heat index high. Wally quits vestibulospinal reflexes lab. Imogene does not sleep. Uh-oh, ketamine.

184.

Patty is sorry to report that things have taken a turn for the better, making her job as a novelist even harder. The ketamine culprit was caught—a Yale sophomore who had broken into Wally's lab, looking for a means to pay for her junior year abroad.

185.

Furthermore, Wally and Imogene are on Imogene's divan.*
(Seated.)

Hours earlier: Imogene had mentioned over the phone that she was getting rid of her knives because they were irreparably dull. Seeing an opportunity, Wally brought over his sharpening kit right away.

186.

The migration of stuff from one abode to another signifies something, does it not?

187.

Yes.

*Nobody knows how to pronounce this word, let alone what it designates.

188.

Wally spent most of the night futilely honing the cleaver before he set aside his bench stone and placed his arm around Imogene. "I like to say my time is money," Wally said, "but in reality it's not." And then they made their way back to the divan. (To sit?)

"Be quiet for a moment," Wally said, putting one hand on Imogene's head, while the other hand roamed until it rested on Imogene's chest, such as it was. "Do you want to know what I am feeling?" Wally said.

189.

Imogene hoped it was not stage four.

"I am feeling that I don't want to keep going without, you know," Wally said.

"Stage forever," thought Imogene. "Do you know why it is I don't have pierced ears?" she said.

Wally did not know.

"Because it's too permanent," said Imogene. Wally nodded his head. Neither of them spoke for a while.

"You should be keeping a list of all the bad things about me," said Imogene.

"I am," said Wally.

Even so, it was quite a night on the divan.

190.

When Wally left the next morning, Imogene wondered if she could use the cleaver to cut tuna melts in two.

191.

From Imogene's, Wally went straight to Derek's so that he could kvell over his achievement and also help Derek set up a wireless webcam because Derek wanted to be able to check the progress of his tomato plants whenever he left home. "You had your hand on one of them and you didn't look?" Derek said with incredulity.

"It's not something I pay attention to," said Wally, assigning the webcam a static IP address on Derek's household intranet.

For those who are, like Derek, curious, but unlike him, too polite to ask, here is a description of the underwear Imogene had on—and off—the night on the divan: Ice-blue front-close Chantilly lace demi-bra with matching boy shorts, adorned with a dainty bow. This set was from the Boy Meets Girl collection.

192.

Style #65.

193.

Unsized sample.

194.

Derek, poor voyeur, will never learn any of this. But perhaps he will find solace in knowing exactly what's doing in his vegetable kingdom.

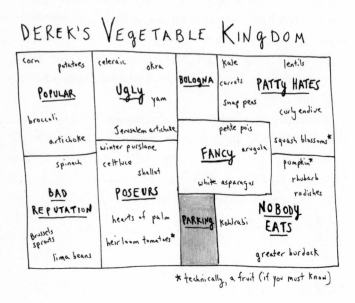

DEREK'S VEGETABLE KINGDOM

* technically, a fruit (if you must know)

195.

Boy oh boy oh boy oh boy. Saks Fifth Avenue.

After Wally said goodbye that morning, Imogene's phone rang. Chalk it up to wishful thinking, self-confidence, or a bad guess, but whatever, Imogene positively expected the caller to be Wally. Before even the exchange of hellos, Imogene said, with an affect that did not suggest nearly as much prurience she'd hoped would be suggested: "Looking for your boxers?"

196.

The caller tittered. "Actually," he said, "I am looking for *your* boxers."

"Excuse me?" Imogene said.

It was Donald Charm from Saks Fifth Avenue. Mr. Charm had seen a pair of Featherware satin bloomers displayed on a blueberry bush in the window of the Blue Tree boutique on Madison Avenue.

Could Imogene come to the office tomorrow to present her spring line?

"Zippity doo-dah," thought Imogene.

197.

"I don't have a spring line," remembered Imogene.

198.

On the topic of making things up:

Imogene wished to spend the night getting her portfolio in tip-top shape. When Wally invited her to a fork-benders exhibition, Imogene said she was very sorry but she had plans.

199.

She was not lying about being sorry.

200.

"You should never make plans," Wally said solemnly.

"Why not?" said Imogene.

"Because then you will always be free to make plans," said Wally.

Did it ever occur to Imogene to tell Wally the truth?

201.

No.

202.

Imogene worked through the night on her packet for Donald Charm. Imogene was most proud of her special-occasion lingerie, which included the Lacy Low Rise Easter panties, the Passover Let My People Go bra, and the April Fools Mesh Surprise.

203.

Imogene ironed every item, for she believed in a crisp presentation.

204.

Imogene always maintained her creaseless standards.

205.

Donald Charm's assistant, a young flibbertigibbet who'd been trying to get chewing gum out of her hair when Imogene arrived, scrunched Imogene's handiwork into a Fed-Ex box. "Sorry," she said, "but something's going on in swimwear and Mr. Charm had to take an emergency holiday in Corfu."

Imogene was disappointed, but it was beneath her to let an assistant know.

"See you," said the assistant. "I mean, don't call. Mr. Charm will e-mail you."

206.

Before anyone knew it, just like that, in a jiffy, Imogene Gilfeather and Wally Yez had set up housekeeping together. The kept house was Imogene's one-and-a-half-bedroom with a wraparound terrace. Which goes to show you—and them, too—that everything is all at once unpredictable and predictable.

207.

Not every single one of Wally's things suited the decor in Imogene's apartment. Those that did not were moved to Wally's pied-à-terre.

208.

Wally has a pied-à-terre?

209.

Not exactly. It was more like a storage space in Long Island City.

210.

No. More like a bin. But, like a pied-à-terre, Wally's bin did have a lock on it.

211.

There was not enough room in chaplette 210 to catalog the contents of Wally's bin.

How about here and now? Sorry, but this chaplette is chock-full of its own meshugas: namely, Patty is presently in litigation, trying to secure permission to inventory Mr. Yez's property. Wally's lawyer, who comes from the world of nonfiction, is arguing that her client should not be deprived of his constitutional right to privacy just because he, the plaintiff, does not quote unquote exist.*

It is unclear what constitutional principle appertains here. To Patty's attorney, anyway.

---

*The judge assigned to *Marx v. Yez* was heard to say recently that he can't help but think Patty's story is enchantingly reminiscent of plenty of other (perfectly legal) stories. For instance, *Don Quixote.*

212.

At any rate, certain belongings of Wally's were found near the bin, having evidently fallen out onto public premises. It is within the author's prerogative to document them. They include lengths of coaxial cable, a turtle toy for Stuffy, a broken motor that Wally kept for heuristic reasons, a decorative flame-thrower, a copy of a movie made in 1920 called *The Future of Pajamas,* a carton labeled "Pieces of String Not Worth Saving," and a big book entitled *Will It Freeze?*

213.

Newly together, Imogene and Wally did what newly togethers do. They marveled at the serendipity that their paths had ever crossed. What were the chances, they said, that both of them would have been at the same going-away party?! And both in the apple pie line?! "What if I had been allergic to pie!" Wally said. "What if Ron de Jean had insisted that he and I leave before dessert!" Imogene said. Wally skirted over this possibility—the mention of another person in his beloved's life was horribly unsettling.

"Immy, what if I had been born in Canada," said Wally, "or the seventeen hundreds?"

Again and again Wally and Imogene rehashed the efflorescing days of their romance. Detail upon detail (see chaplettes 1, 3, 7, 8, 10, 12, 16, 17, 20, 26, 27, 28, &c.). They asked each other how did you feel when I said that, what did you think was going to happen when that happened, had you ever imagined such a person as I.

214.

They offered commentary.

215.

They were pundits about themselves.

216.

Storytellers about their story.

217.

They tried to dream about each other. Wally was successful. They kept odd hours. Imogene's were odder. They went to the movies and didn't pay attention to the screen. They went grocery shopping and brought home the wrong bags. They left notes for each other inside the strangest places—medicine cabinets, mailboxes, butter dishes, ziplock-storage bags, socks. They tried out different terms of endearment. Nothing sounded natural enough. They said, give it time, the right names will come to us.

218.

They both liked broccoli.

219.

They both used mechanical pencils (not the same make, but still).

220.

They agreed about paper towels.

221.

Growing up, neither had had a dog nor mumps.

222.

Both had a mother who stayed up all hours, and a father who went to bed early.

223.

Neither had been to Istanbul.

224.

They were so alike, weren't they? It was uncanny, they said.

She loved to watch him listen to jazz. He adored the way she played with a particular strand of her hair. She now thought the half-moons on his thumbnails were the most beautiful half-moons she had ever seen. He was enamored with her habit of sitting cross-legged. He got a charge every time she pronounced the word *strawberry*. She was partial to his slight overbite.

No, they never tired of each other. They had not heard all of each other's anecdotes yet.

And when they were with friends—not in the company of each other—they coaxed the conversation to a place where, for instance, they could interject, "Wally has an aunt who was a spy" or "That reminds me, Imogene once found a letter from Daniel Patrick Moynihan in a library book."

There was always something to celebrate! The five-month anniversary of the first time they touched each other on purpose, the three-month anniversary of the first time they took public transportation together, the two-day anniversary of the first time they saw each other with wet hair, the seven-month, three-week, two-day, four-hour anniversary of when Wally really *knew*.

They liked to reminisce about the instant that just went by.

225.

The Happy Days. (Say no more.)

226.

They were so happy, friends stayed away.

227.

Who was the first to be unhappy (not counting Patty)?

228.

As usual, there is no clue in the haiku:

> *The jonquil petals*
> *Cicada's cry in moonlight.*
> *Sad strappy sandals?*

229.

How about in the skywriting?

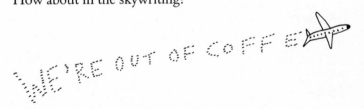

230.

In other boroughs, Mrs. Schine's boy married the wrong girl, Mr. del Gaizo's keys fell through a subway grate, Victoria R. Pepall did not get everything she'd hoped for in the will, Suzzy Hamblen's fine sheets were destroyed by Taiwanese hot water bottles, fledgling actors in high school productions forgot their lines, waiters refused substitutions, subjects and verbs disagreed (to put it mildly), frogs were dying as were the bees, and life was no fucking bowl of cherries (for Patty either).

231.

Things improve.

232.

Sometimes.

233.

For others.

234.

"He asked me to marry him," Imogene said to Harriet. Imogene and Harriet were working late, designing samples for the new Featherware-able line.

"Oh my God, oh my God, oh my God, shouldn't we go out for champagne or omelets or something?" said Harriet. Imogene, who was intent on stretching a shred of black Lycra across the derriere of a mannequin, seemed not to hear a word.

"Did you see the scissors?" Imogene said, looking around. "They were just here."

"Here," said Harriet, handing her boss the scissors. "When did he ask? Tell me everything."

"This morning," said Imogene, "while I was flossing my teeth." Imogene snipped away at the Lycra, and then twisted what remained of the fabric around the girth of the mannequin.

"That is so romantic," said Harriet. "Did he knock, or just walk in and look at you flossing and then you just knew?" Harriet liked to get the whole picture.

Imogene remembered maybe half the picture. She daintily rolled the edges of the underpants. "Voilà. The Anti-Thong," Imogene said with pride. "What do you think? Don't you think it's about time for women to accentuate, not hide, their visible panty line?"

"I guess it is," said Harriet. "What did you say when Wally asked? You said yes, right?"

"First I finished flossing my teeth," said Imogene, "and then I said no."

The Anti-Thong
with Protruding LED Bands

235.

Imogene fussed with her creation. "We could put piping around the edges, of course," Imogene said.

"Or take a risk with rickrack!" said Harriet.

236.

Imogene's phone rang. It was Wally.

237.

Wally had had an origami accident.

"Why are you calling me?" said Imogene—not peeved, just curious. "Shouldn't you be looking for a Band-Aid?" Imogene gestured to Harriet that she'd be off the phone presently. To Wally she said, "The Band-Aids are on the bottom shelf of the bathroom cabinet."

"I just wanted to hear your voice," said Wally. "It's really deep," he said, referring to his wound.

"What's deep?" said Imogene, afraid of the possibilities.

It was fortunate that Imogene's Serapi carpet had a tawny-colored background.

"Wal, hearing my voice is not going to fix anything," said Imogene. "I think you better take care of your finger right away." She gestured *sorry about this* to Harriet.

"I didn't expect you to fix anything," said Wally. "I feel better just talking to you. It's soothing. Could I tell you some thoughts I had about you today?"

"Write them down, can't you?" said Imogene, pointing to

the halter top in Harriet's right hand because the darts on the halter top in Harriet's other hand would flatter no bosom.

"Ow," said Wally.

"Do you want me to take you to the hospital?" said Imogene, who preferred fixing to soothing.

"No, thank you," said Wally, "it's not an emergency anymore."

The phone call was concluded. Imogene resumed business, but she'd definitely been touched. She wondered if Wally had cribbed any of his thoughts about her from the Lake Poets.

(Little-known fact: tapioca pudding with a pinch of powdered ginger works wonders on carpets.)

238.

At breakfast, the next morning, Wally said to Imogene, who was kneeling on the rug, "Could you please not spray toxic chemicals while I'm eating?"

239.

In what might be called the middle of the night, Imogene gently jabbed Wally awake. "There is something I need to tell you," she said. "It's very important."

Wally turned toward her and smiled. "Yes?" he said, in happy anticipation.

"I don't believe there's such a thing as compromise," she said. "It's just the winner's way of saying 'no hard feelings' to the loser."

Wally pulled Imogene closer. "We'll each compromise fifty percent of the time," he said. "No ifs, ands, or buts."

Verbs Patty Almost Used Instead of "Jab"

Verb	Likelihood
poke	3%
prod	2%
stab	3%
clobber	4%
maul	5%
nudge	1%
thump	6%
bite	4%
bully	3%
percuss	12%
cluck	1.3%
smoke	6%
monetize	8%
jub	40.7%

240.

Wally and Imogene swore that they would tell each other everything. No secrets, they said. Forever. Wally looked at Imogene adoringly. Then they had nothing to say.

"Did I ever tell you about when I sold part of my Bulgarian stamp collection?" said Wally.

241.

When the package arrived, Wally wasted no time tearing it open. "I can't believe you got those things," said Imogene, who was theoretically minding her own business.

"I know," said Wally, in enthusiastic agreement. "Wait, what things?"

"Those," said Imogene, indicating the many boxes of individually wrapped toothpicks Wally had just received.

"They're just what I wanted!" he said. "Now I don't have to keep swiping them from the diner."

"But twelve thousand?" said Imogene, who'd put down her magazine to get a closer look.

"Let's say I go through five a day—conservatively," said Wally, with deliberation. "That's one thousand, eight hundred twenty-five a year."

"Wally," said Imogene.

"Are you saying I should order more?" said Wally. "They were only thirteen dollars. The price will definitely go up. What if we order a million?"

What Imogene was saying, though she did not say it, was that having one's apartment burgled had its upside.

Wally cracked open a box of toothpicks, and handed one to Imogene. "We can give them as Christmas presents," he said. "To people who eat."

Imogene unwrapped a toothpick and held it up to the light. "It does seem awfully well made," she mused.

Wally beamed. "We agree about the important things," he said, reaching for her hand. "Will you marry me?"

242.

Sometimes the best things come in small packages, and sometimes things just come in packages.

243.

That night at dinner, Imogene said, "Nobody's kid got into college today." Wally helped himself to seconds. Imogene said, "If we had a kid, where do you think it wouldn't get in?"

Wally put down his fork. "Our kid?" Wally said. "Our kid would not get into Harvard!"

Imogene smiled. Wally reached across the table for the salt. "Will you marry me?" he said.

"Oh, wait," she said. "The brat in 12D got wait-listed at Tufts."

244.

How Wally Spent His Summer Vacation,
Except for One Week

245.

How Imogene Spent Her Summer Vacation,
Except for One Week

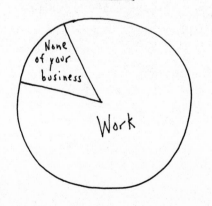

246.

Then came the week that cannot be graphed. Imogene and Wally visited a charming metropolis in Europe. They never made it to the cathedral, but they agreed to tell friends and family how they'd been especially taken with the stained glass in one of those side rooms—were they called sacristies? Imogene and Wally did see the public gardens. The flowers were in self-important bloom, especially the lavender. Imogene didn't get the point of lingering there once they'd looked around. Wally went to the police museum and ran through the war museum, or was it the other way around? Meanwhile, Imogene shopped for lace. Look at the light, they said to each other so many times that they were scared they'd never be able to quit saying it. They were sick of the light, too. Naturally, they ate well. Imogene was pleased she hadn't gained weight. All that walking, they both theorized. How many kilograms in a pound again? Imogene thought. Oh, and finally, they almost missed their return flight because Wally spent a terrifically long time trying to decide if he should put the foreign coins in his pocket or pack them in the suitcase. "It's all the same," said Imogene finally. "That's what makes it an impossible decision," said Wally.

247.

All in all, they had a really lovely week.

248.

Wally and Imogene were still crazy about each other—even after their luggage was lost. As they waited for the man at the counter to return with the lost-baggage forms, Wally took Imogene's hand. "Do you realize how close I came to putting the coins in my medium-sized soft upright?" he said, pointing to the chart of suitcase types that were possible to lose.

249.

When Wally and Imogene got home, everyone asked if they'd had nice weather. "It rained," said Imogene. Everyone seemed to take it badly. Nobody asked about the cathedral. Maybe everyone was just too dismayed about the meteorological conditions.

250.

Imogene's mind was still elsewhere.

293.

Patty meant 251. But Patty likes the ring of 293.

294.

Here's a thought: Could it be that Patty, with your reading pleasure in mind, had slyly deleted the chaplettes particularly heavy in detailia of Imogene and Wally cleaning closets, filing taxes, renewing passports, defrosting the freezer even though it was supposed to be too modern for that, buying a quart of 2%, figuring out how to get there, waiting for the light to turn green, fast-forwarding through the commercials, adjusting the knob, calling the wrong number, being on hold, hello goodbye, buttoning the buttons, zipping the zips, smelling their hands?

Or could Patty be tiptoeing past some unpleasantness in chaplettes 251–292?

Prosaic truth: Patty meant 293. Numbering is harder than you think. Everything is.

295.

Wally Yez and Imogene Gilfeather lived together under the same roof for several more months until one day, a year had gone by.

296.

Then there was more of the same.

297.

(The following chaplette is the recipient of the 2011 Hyundai Prize, awarded biannually to the most outstanding work of literature written and revised while driving.)

Et cetera, et cetera, et cetera.

298.

Wally had meant to celebrate their anniversary with a surprise Imogene would never forget, but by the time Wally remembered the milestone, the statute of limitations for commemorations had passed. If Wally can forget a triumphant date like this, nobody's safe.

299.

There follows a transcript of a conversation that took place in Imogene and Wally's living room, a little after chaplette 298.

300.

IMOGENE: I thought you said you were going to take out the trash.

WALLY: Here's the secret about me. If you want me to take out the trash, you have to put it by the front door.

IMOGENE: That's the secret?

WALLY: Yes. So don't tell anyone or everyone will start leaving their trash there.

IMOGENE: Wally!

WALLY: What?

IMOGENE: I'm going to make some toast, read the paper, empty the dishwasher, and file my nails. Meanwhile, will you take out the trash?

WALLY: That's the difference between you and me. You're a doer, and I'm more of a can-do type.

301.

Lo, one night, the crazy lady in 7G was taken away in an ambulance, never to return. Imogene made an inquiry.

303.*

There were already three bids on the apartment.
    (Come on, this is New York!)

CCCIV.

Not Rome.

*Editor's Note: Chaplette 302 can be found in Volume 4 of Will and Ariel Durant's *The Story of Civilization*.

305.

Wally fixed the thingamajig inside the television! He was even more astonished than Imogene by his aptitude. "It took me a long time to learn I was a fast learner," he said.

"Isn't that what you said the first time I talked to you on the phone—when you fixed my computer?" said Imogene.

"If it was," said Wally, "then I agree with myself."

306.

Eventually, there came a time (inevitable, isn't it?) when Imogene felt comfortable enough with Wally to let her hair down, all but a wayward strand. One day, when Imogene's hair was not only recklessly down, but unstyled, Wally said, "Imo, do you want to walk over to the gallery with the neon sign? They're having an opening of the sculptor you liked at the museum that time."

Imogene said yes, but shouldn't she at least comb her hair?

Wally said, "Oh, your hair looks fine enough for an exhibit that takes place in the basement gallery. But you might want to put on some lipstick or something, and on second thought, comb your hair."

A few blocks from the gallery, Wally happened to mention that his friends Derek, Jonathan, Thomas, Gerry, Matthew, Michael, Rick, and Nino, and maybe Wally's old girlfriend, might be at the opening. Well, probably they would, he said. They would. Definitely.

Imogene turned around and marched home.

307.

It was one thing to appear among strangers when your hair is down, but another thing to do it near neon.

308.

Who is wrong?
　　Wally or Imogene?
　　(This is the question this story is posing.)

309.

Another question, this one posed by Patty:
　　Are you really going to finish that?

310.

Imogene and Wally went to brunch at the Sepkowitzes'. Wally did most of the talking, a fair share of the eating, a lot of the laughing, a respectable amount of the clearing plates from the table, and all of the legerdemain. When the other guests got up to go, Wally and Imogene stayed. They stayed even after Imogene politely mentioned to Wally that it was long past brunchtime, let alone lunchtime. And besides, she had stuff to do.

"Oh, don't go," said Meg Sepkowitz. "There's more Bloody Mary mix."

"Just a few more minutes," said Wally to Imogene. At long last, Imogene and Wally put on their coats and took their umbrellas. Imogene opened the front door. "Wow," said Wally, taking in the portrait of Richard Sepkowitz and Meg Sepkowitz hanging in the vestibule. "You guys sure were lucky to find a painting that looked just like you." The Sepkowitzes laughed.

311.

"Wally is a big Yes," said Richard. "And Imogene is a big No."

312.

Everyone, even Imogene, seemed to find that enchantingly droll.

313.

The observation deserves repeating. Wally is a big Yes and Imogene is a big No.

314.

Wally and Imogene were but a block from the Sepkowitzes' when Wally said, "At some point I was trying to figure out if I was the fattest person in the room."

The author does not consider Wally fat, but there is no denying that between chaplettes 198 and 233, Wally had put on weight. Imogene did not reply. She had her own weight to think of.

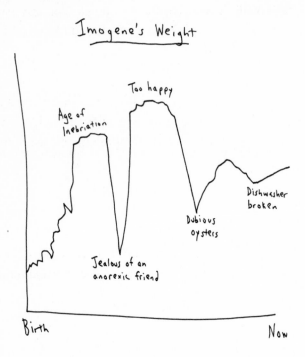

315.

It has dawned on the author that heretofore in these pages, the word *droll* has been used twice. Furthermore, in her lifetime, Patty has milked the word *enchantingly* dry. In light of this, let the official record, in the fourth revision, show that everyone seemed to find Richard Sepkowitz's remark waggishly apt.

316.

Tragically so.

317.

On the way home, Imogene did not want to marry Wally again, and said so. Wally put his finger through the belt loop of Imogene's trench coat and pulled her toward him. He was not a quitter.

318.

"One more question," said Wally. "Do you think we'll be in this book long enough for them to hear me stop pleading with you?"

319.

Enough horsing around.

320.

Back at the Sepkowitzes', the party was over and Meg and Richard were combing the living room for stray glasses and dessert plates to take back to the kitchen. "Don't Imogene and Wally remind you of Elizabeth Bennet and Mr. Darcy?" said Richard.

"Let me think," said Meg, who was doing a cost-benefit analysis of whether it was worth it to cork up a nearly empty bottle of champagne. "Which would be which?" she said, taking a swig to finish up the bubbly.

321.

Soon it would be Wally's birthday. When Imogene suggested they have a birthday party, Wally agreed with gusto. "Let's see," said Imogene, thinking of the guest list. "Who is your favorite person?" "You," said Wally. "Who are your two favorites, then?" said Imogene. "You and the person you used to be," said Wally.

322.

When Wally read the news in the obits, he was delivered of a noise loud enough to bring Imogene into the room at a brisk pace. "This can't be!" he said. "He was only thirty-four—oh, that's someone else. He was ninety." Wally put his head in his hands. "I need to let this sink in." The father of Chaos Theory had died, and Wally appeared distraught.

"Did you know him?" said Imogene in a tone that could be called sympathetic. She pulled up a chair.

"Frankly, I didn't even know he was alive," said Wally, lifting his head. He read further. "Wow, they're equating him with Newton, and that's crap."

Imogene stood up. "You got over his death awfully fast," she observed.

"You know what the Stages of Grief woman neglected to realize?" said Wally. "That the last stage is happiness."

"Sometimes the first stage, too," said Imogene, wondering if chaos were ahead. "I'll speak at your funeral if you speak at mine," she said as she left the room, but Wally did not seem to hear.

323.

Or maybe he did.

324.

He didn't look happy.

325.

Wally could have gone for a scalp massage right about now, but Elsie was in Montana at the ranch of a client whose mule was apparently in pressing need of a perm. "Wish you were here," she'd written on a postcard Wally received not long ago. "P.S. Do you know how to use bear spray?" "P.P.S. Answer asap."

326.

It would not be something anyone could predict, but Wally showed more conscientiousness with regard to washing the dishes than Imogene did. On this particular night, however, Wally asked Imogene after dinner if it would be okay with her if he left the casserole dish in the sink overnight to soak. Yes, it would be okay.

"What would you have said if I'd said no?" said Imogene much later.

"I would have removed the dish from the sink," said Wally, "because in this house, you come before pots and pans." Imogene looked at Wally charitably. Wally continued. "But *after* neodymium magnets."

327.

Let's put it this way. Wally's ex has had a baby. Let's put it another way. Patty agrees with Wally and the rest of the world that Trench is not a felicitous name for a child. Or anything. Except possibly a trench. Or a disease of the mouth.

328.

Wally, who is, in general, happy for everyone, was not, in particular, happy for Gwen. Call it babyish, but Wally was jealous. Reproduction, as every scientist knows, is a fundamental feature of life. Not only that: offspring mean cartoons, Halloween candy, and little toes.

But Wally did not want anyone's baby. He most trenchantly did not want Gwen's.

"What do ounces have to do with it?" Wally whined to his intended when he read the birth announcement.

"Babies," said Imogene. "They are the worst kind of houseguest."

329.

Imogene was not convinced that propagating was the most affordable gift she could give society. Moreover, she was suspicious of her genes. Based on photographic albums and anecdotes from Pop Pop and Aunt Mimma, here is the way she pictured her forebears, the stock she took of her stock:

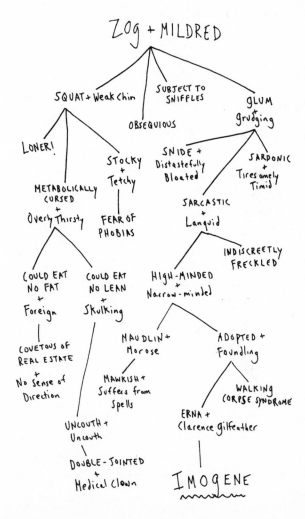

329a.

Wally's pedigree needs no tree-ing, but fair is fair (sometimes):

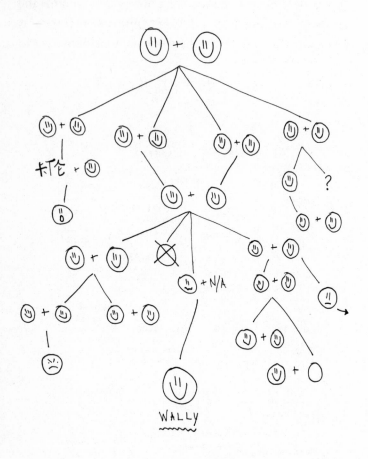

WALLY

330.

Breaking news: Ron de Jean and his missus split up. Imogene didn't see it coming, but everyone else did. This is not one of those books where the author is surprised by what her characters do.

331.

When Imogene told Wally that she was going to a bistro that night with Ron de Jean, Wally remembered that, long ago, he had asked Imogene about Ron de Jean, and she had insisted the romance between them was kaput. Is that what she'd said? Can anyone be held accountable for what they said far back in chaplette 17?

"But the peak of the Perseids meteor shower is tonight," Wally moaned. "The conditions for viewing may never be as optimal in our lifetime. I had my heart set on watching with you."

"We'll just have to live longer, Wal," said Imogene, grabbing her jacket. "I'm late."

332.

Ron de Jean did not see what was so wrong about it. He and Imogene were merely having a bite at a nice but not too nice café. There was less than one bottle of wine involved and the lighting was un-dim. They were not at a corner table. Nobody ordered oysters, truffles, or anything like that. There was no gazing into each other's eyes. They confessed nothing, they promised nothing. When the waiter asked about dessert or coffee, neither Ron de Jean nor Imogene said, "Not for me, but why don't you have something so that we can linger?" They split the check.

Another reason Ron de Jean saw nothing wrong: he had designs on a foot model whose most fetching physical features were situated above her pedal extremities.

333.

Imogene saw nothing wrong either. Leave Wally for Ron de Jean? She was not that enterprising. Nor was she in the mood for having a frank talk or putting things, hers or Wally's, in cartons. Besides, Ron de Jean was just a guy she'd known forever, having met him one summer when, as a way of making money and staying cool, she posed as a model in a life-drawing class. Ron de Jean was the keenest of students.

334.

Wally could see things that others could not.

335.

In the middle of his turmoil, Wally, who had been fretting at home, decided to get right up and go to an all-night drugstore to shop for a pair of scissors. He studied all the scissors. "Can I give you a word of advice?" said a customer in the store, who'd gone for a heated pair. "Never skimp on a scissors."

Obviously this man did not know Wally. Wally was many things, but he was not a skimper.

336.

Wüsthof Grand Prix Kitchen Shears, $50.95. Do not use on large poultry.

337.

Wally spent the better part of the next day trying to decide whether to go to a bachelor party that night (old friends, free whiskey, possible ride home) versus stay home (100 percent chance of precipitation, Celtics vs. Knicks, Imogene). "Tell me what to do," Wally said to Imogene.

"Go," she said, with no apparent reflection, not even looking up from her crocheting. Imogene had other things on her mind (rye toast, mmm).

"You're not being helpful," said Wally. "Helpful would be if you said don't go—if you said, please, whatever you do, don't go."

"Really?" said Imogene. (What did he say?)

338.

The next night, Wally and Imogene were in bed when Wally said, "If I died, how sad would you be?" Imogene put down her sketchbook. "On a scale of five to eighteen," said Wally.

"Are fractions allowed?" she said.

"Seriously," said Wally. "What would you do?"

Imogene looked around the room. She said she would really throw herself into cleaning the apartment.

"Maybe that's a good way to get the apartment cleaned," said Wally.

(Is eighteen the most or least sad?)

(How sad would the reader be? Please express the answer in milligrams.)

339.

Tears dribbled down Wally's face, but Imogene never knew it, for, at the same time, in the same bed, she was dropping artificial lubricant into her chronically dry eyes.

Imogene turned out the lights.

340.

Imogene closed her eyes and pretended she was at the eye doctor's. To pass the time while she fake-waited to get her eyes fake-dilated, Imogene composed an alphabetic mental list of the friends of hers who'd never reciprocated with a gift equal to or better than the one she had given first.

She got up to her friend Lisa (paper napkins) before nodding off.

341.

Wally dreams about Imogene every night. Sometimes she turns into someone else and sometimes she takes a shuttle to a place where Wally knows she's going to die. Usually, Wally's dreams are nightmares. Tonight, he is on a mudslide being chased by zombies. Imogene tries to help him, but then it turns out she is trying to kill him. Then she accidentally—or not—kicks him, and he wakes up before he kills her.

342.

Imogene does not have time for dreams right now. Let us, then, look to her penmanship. Some say it is her most admirable attribute.

343.

A sample of Imogene's handwriting, along with a graphological analysis.

Could you pick up paper towels (not floral) when you're out?

Imo

Note the excessive straightness of the baseline, a sign that the writer is tense and overly disciplined. Pay attention as well to the verticality of the lettering—that is, no leftward or rightward slantitude. This suggests that the writer is self-sufficient, tries to keep her emotions in check, and may possibly be considered cold and uncaring. The darkness of the script indicates that great pressure was exerted, the mark of someone who has supreme vitality, is usually highly successful and/or berserk. Let us contrast Imogene's cursive with Wally's scribble (see below).

The writer forms strong loops in the lower zone, which shows a desire for sex, food, money, and shiny objects. The loop on the *l* is high and narrow—a sign of idealism. The open-topped *o* could mean that this person cannot keep a secret, whereas the shape of the crossbar on the *t* suggests that this person surely knows the meaning of mum's the word. The high squiggly exclamation points show a vivid imagination or the influence of alcohol. We have never seen a *k* like this.

Only a single example of the author's handwriting is said to exist. Unaccountably, her signature was found on a petition from May 1987, requisitioning the tearing down of an opera house.

If Patty's signature were an EKG, the patient flatlined by the second syllable.

344.

When Beenish invited Wally to the launch of Dollar and Change Kabab, he went with honorable and hungry intentions. When Beenish bounded toward Wally and threw her arms around him, he got right to the point. "I've plighted my troth to Imogene," he said, taking a step backward.

"Wow," said Beenish, taking a step forward. "Really?"

"No, not exactly, but more or less," said Wally. Beenish started to cry. "Less," said Wally. They stood still.

Beenish took Wally's arm and wiped her eyes on his sleeve. "I have an idea," began Beenish.

Where was Imogene? She was at the co-op meeting, opining about water seepage on the north facade.

345.

Beenish Asif's plan entailed no biotechnology. Biology, she was confident, would take care of everything.

Beenish already had a name picked out. If it were a boy, Yakub after her uncle; and if it were a girl, Doris Day after Doris Day. If, however, Wally had a suggestion, Beenish would be pleased to consider it.

It was a perfect plan, she thought, incorporating everything she desired: someone to eat for, followed in nine months by someone to play with (who has good toys).

346.

Plan B: see Plan A (above).

347.

When Wally returned home, he woke up Imogene. "Do you want a baby?" Wally said. She opened her eyes a peep and nodded no.

"How about part of one?" Wally said, but Imogene had already fallen back asleep. "I've made a decision," he said nonetheless. "I'm not going to let you get rid of me."

Imogene was dreaming of Wally's socks.

348.

The next day, it was resolved by Wally and Imogene that the plan could never fly. Too rough on a child. Too avant-garde. Imogene wanted no role. She did not want to be called aunt or auntimo. She detested baby talk. The apartment would be a mess. Imogene had a nice carpet, don't forget. She had her career, remember. What if the kid had problems or bad manners? What if it reached the third grade and read on a second-grade level? There was a possibility that it would never have a playmate. What if Wally didn't feel like throwing around a ball? What if Beenish wanted to raise it as a creationist? Some teenagers murder their parents. Or worse—don't clean up their rooms. We could never tolerate a bad report card. Would we be expected at PTA meetings? Would Beenish? Which one of us would be a volunteer crossing guard? Imogene thought she did not look good in yellow vinyl, and Wally slept late, but could they both shirk responsibility? What if we didn't approve of the prom date? We couldn't allow a minor to choose the college. How many guests would we be allowed to invite to the wedding? What would Imogene tell her mother? We'd need a spare room. We'd need a lawyer. There goes our trip to Istanbul. It would impinge on our bliss. It would cost a lot of money. Scads and scads.

"And besides," said Wally, "I would never want an off-spring who did not remind me of you."

"Thank you," said Imogene. "But really, go ahead."

"No," said Wally. "I don't think I want to be part of a threesome."

"A foursome," said Imogene.

349.

Wally and Imogene returned to their life.

350.

They had cereal for dinner.

351.

"But why aren't you jealous?" Wally said, tapping the over-turned box to coax out the last of the recalcitrant toasted wheat flakes. "I would be jealous," Wally said.

"Please pass the milk," said Imogene.

"I *am* jealous," thought Wally.

352.

Wally gave Imogene a soulful look.

353.

Wally went to New Jersey for a conference entitled "Why Darwin Just Had to Naturally Select Emma Wedgwood." When, after many days, Wally showed up at home again, Imogene looked up from her sewing and remembered how she'd felt about him in the days before she knew him intimately, if she really did.

She felt a frisson of *je ne sais quoi.*

354.

"So," she said, "is it nature or nurture?"

"Norture," said Wally, opening the refrigerator. "Leftover Mexican or leftover Indian?"

"Neither," said Imogene. "Not even Indican."

355.

That settled that.*

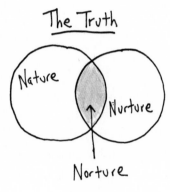

356.

While Wally was waiting for his dungarees to dry in the dryer, he took an online career aptitude test. "Guess my dream career!" he said, marching into Imogene's office with the exciting news. His dungarees were still damp.

"Just a moment," said Imogene. "I'm trying to write a memo."

"But we were in the middle of a conversation," said Wally.

---

*In the Russian edition of this book, misleadingly entitled *Doctor Zhivago,* Wally replies, "Torture," not "Norture."

357.

Imogene went back to writing her memo.*

358.

Wally kneaded Imogene's shoulder. He did not tell her that according to métiermatch.com, he was a person who liked to go with the flow, act before thinking, live for the moment (but also for what will be), explain things with big words, and freeze, not burn, to death. Nor did he tell her that he, like Robert Oppenheimer and Joan of Arc, would find fulfillment, happiness, and reward as a shepherd in New Zealand. He did not tell Imogene that he'd also filled out the questionnaire on her behalf, and she should absolutely pursue a life of petty crime.

Instead, Wally said to Imogene, "Do you know how lucky you are to have someone who loves you as much as I do? That's worth many hundreds of dollars a year."

359.

Here's the thing: Imogene did.

*In the Inuit edition of this book, endearingly entitled *Ukluk Learns to Dog Sled,* Wally (Ukluk) clops into Imogene's (K'eyghasthuntu's) igloo, and says something we don't understand because we don't speak Inuit. Nobody really does.

360.

The next time Wally asked Imogene to marry him, she polled a bunch of her girlfriends to find out how happy they were in their marriages. "It's nice to have someone around who'll get things off of the high shelves," e-mailed a woman thrice married to increasingly taller men. "And you are never locked out of the house for long."

"I'm content," said another respondent. "But if Mark spontaneously incinerated, I wouldn't marry again. Would I marry Mark again? You're joking! Are you joking?"

"Happy?" a newlywed told Imogene. "That's such a nondescriptive description. It's more like miserable. I miss my lonely Saturday nights."

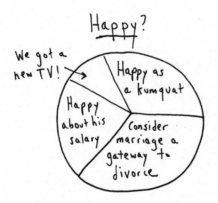

Indeed, the results were not a hip-hip-hooray for wedlock, though there was emphatic support for the convenience of two people sharing entrées at Chinese restaurants.

361.

Mathematical psychologists have determined the marital bliss quotient to be uncannily close to π.

362.

Wally sent Imogene a postcard, enumerating her virtues (the usuals, plus spelling), declaring his everlasting love for her, and calling her attention to the fact that he could have handed her the epistle that morning in the kitchen, but felt that his gratuitous expenditure on postage would prove the degree of his amour.*

363.

One beautiful day, Wally told Imogene that he thought evaporation was overrated. Imogene was not aware that evaporation had been rated.

364.

"See that parking lot?" Wally said to Imogene one day while they were hurrying to get somewhere. "I parked there once."

"That's nice," said Imogene, who was trying to remember if she liked clementines or was it tangelos.

---

*In the Irish version of this book, *Athbhliain Faoi Mhaise Duit,* Wally takes a drink.

"And now you know everything about me," said Wally. "That's all there is."

"Clementines," thought Imogene.

The PARKING PLACES of WALLY YEZ

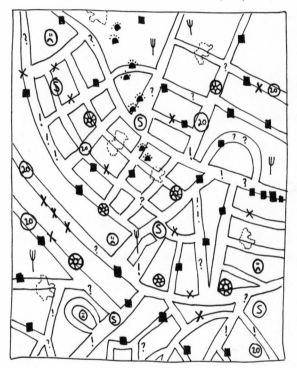

KEY

- ■ Illegal
- ? Legalish
- Ψ Reserved for visiting chefs
- Ⓐ Emotionally handicapped parking
- ✕ Backbiting, double-crossing meters
- ! Fun meter

- ⑳ Twenty second parking
- Ⓢ Stowaway zone
- ✹ Rollaway zone
- ⟳ Sinkhole
- ⁖ Turtle crossing
- Invisible hydrant

365.

There were times that Wally or Imogene would think, prior to replying to the other: What words does my beloved most want to hear? There were other times when each would think: What could I say that would result in the most vexation?

366.

But mostly there was the rest of the time.

367.

In the European Paintings and Sculpture wing, Wally and Imogene lost each other, though which had been the loser and which had been lost was never determined.

368.

How about a break from these people with their needs and their desires and their Sturm und the other word and their yakkety-yak?

369.

Patty's really sorry. She was thinking of characters in another book. A musical interlude is in order.

370.

Despite chaplette 367, Wally slept soundly.

371.

"And loudly," thought Imogene.

372.

Maybe he did and maybe he didn't. Patty was not there.
Patty has a life to live, you know.

373.

Sort of.

374.

Imogene watched Wally breathe for a good long while, and finally she thought about this person lying an arm's length away in her bed. She thought: "Is that a cowlick? Does he really have a cowlick? If yes, no bed will ever be big enough."

375.

Imogene had the bed to herself the next night, and there was palpable emptiness in the closets, cabinets, and commode, too. That morning, at a punishing hour, Wally had said goodbye, off to go camping with a group of his chums. He was to be gone for thirty-six hours, but had packed enough stuff to supply himself into eternity. "Why aren't you worried I'll be eaten by a mountain lion?" Wally asked Imogene, his voice breaking.

Imogene yawned. "Isn't it bears that eat people?" she said.

376.

On Day #2, Imogene had a nettlesome thought: Why had Wally put a jacket and a tie into his duffel? Camping trips could turn apocalyptic, but they rarely require business attire.

377.

Boy Scouts motto: Be Prepared!

378.

Ready for the ritornello of Ron de Jean? Imogene's dishwasher was broken, and who else could fix it? Ron de Jean knew as much about servicing a float switch as Robespierre did about half-court basketball. Neither could hold a candle to Wally, who was a man who knew his water inlet valves. Wally, however, was in the woods. *Que sera.*

"Thanks for thinking of me," said Ron de Jean when he walked through the door, his arms outstretched. The foot model Ron de Jean had a crush on had recently crushed his heart.

"I was thinking of myself," Imogene said.

Ron de Jean took it the nondishwasher way.

379.

"The rule about home repair," said Ron de Jean, backing away from the leaky machine, "is first do no harm."

380.

With that, he and Imogene withdrew to the living room, where they were on the verge of retiring to the bedroom when Ron de Jean's daughter called to say that Lauren's mother forgot to pick them up from skating so could he please hurry and get them.

381.

It was not an auspicious moment as moments go.

382.

In retrospect, Imogene was filled with rue, but she was not sure what the rue was on account of.

383.

"It is definitely not just like old times," Imogene thought.
    It never is, is what Patty says.

384.

When Wally returned home, Imogene was in the middle of a lively phone call—about the effect of globalization on

Indonesian polyester. Imogene held up a finger, signaling she would be off in a finger's amount of time.

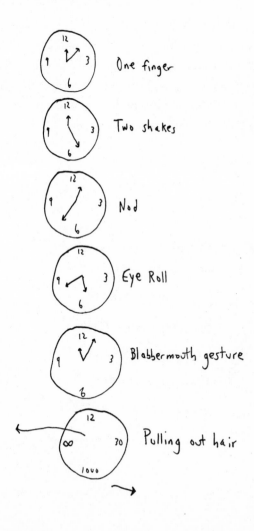

Guide to Time on the Phone

One finger

Two shakes

Nod

Eye Roll

Blabbermouth gesture

Pulling out hair

385.

But she wasn't.

386.

As moments go, it was long. The conversation drifted to a spirited one about pancake recipes. "You don't like me," said Wally after Imogene hung up. "You feel everything I do is wrong, and you are wondering, what are you doing spending your life with me."

Imogene's Idea

Sorry. The recipe for "Pick-Me-Up Whiskey Pancakes" was removed by Patty's editor who says there are already too many recipes in books.

387.

A moment of silence now for Ron de Jean, who died on the squash court reaching for what turned out to be a deadly shot. In lieu of condolences, please send contributions to the Hastings-on-Hudson Save the Receipts Foundation.

388.

Imogene had never been prouder to "know" Ron de Jean, for there is no more fabulous celebrity than the dead person at a funeral. Until everybody goes home.

During a eulogy in which it was claimed Ron de Jean had been a bon vivant, husband and father extraordinaire, shoulder to cry on, modern dance aficionado, connoisseur of marmalade, humanitarian, and minor saint, Imogene received a text message saying that Donald Charm from Saks Fifth Avenue had approved her proposal and would be buying one thousand units of Featherware underclothing. Saks wanted an exclusive on Lethal, Imogene's teen line! And Barely Lethal, her preteen line!

Imogene was too happy to be sad.

389.

Isn't life something!

390.

When you're not dead.

391.

The next day, upon Imogene's suggestion, she and Wally decided they should buy an apartment together. They had their eyes on a classic six that they were sure would go for a song because of the blood. Also, the wallpaper in the second bathroom was bowling-themed.

392.

Some people like packing.

393.

Some people like unpacking.

394.

Imogene didn't particularly like either packing or unpacking, but she was more fastidious than Wally, so here she was, trying to organize their new place. Mountains and mesas, caves and lava streams of labeled cardboard boxes remained unexplored, let alone unconquered. Imogene surveyed the terrain of the master bedroom, trying to imagine future habitation.

395.

Imogene knew exactly where she would have put the outlets if they weren't already where they spitefully were.

396.

Later, as Imogene contemplated the linen closet, Wally breezed in, home from work early and brandishing a bottle of champagne. Imogene hoped he'd gotten a raise, but she did not ask. "Im, I have some really great news." Maybe he'd succeeded in synthesizing that protein. Wasn't that what he was trying to do? Or was it an enzyme? But aren't enzymes proteins? Either way it was good news.

397.

For proteins.

398.

"I'm going to have a baby!" said Wally with widened eyes. "I can't *not* have progeny, can I?"

"Whose?" said Imogene, her attention on the washcloths. "Can you reach that shelf up there?" Imogene said.

"Yours," said Wally. "You think I'm kidding. I'm not kidding."

"Ha ha ha ha," said Imogene.

399.

Wally could reach the shelf.

400.

"Fine," said Imogene. Who wasn't kidding now? Imogene tried to concentrate on the bedding. If she were not shrewd about arranging the sheets and towels—put the pillowcases on the second shelf instead of on the third shelf?—it would be wrong forever. Nobody reorders their linen closet. She considered her choices. Was that impending doom she sensed?

401.

"I'm having a baby with you," said Wally. "So you better get used to it. You're going to have a lot of diaper changing to do because I have a lot to do at work." Wally smiled, even though, as he said, he was not kidding.

Wally did not open the champagne bottle.

402.

One and all were taken by surprise when Wally and Imogene parted ways. What had happened? Rumors simmered, then burbled, then percolated, then splashed all over town.

403.

It was an insuperable mess.

404.

They said Wally had knocked up his Pakistani girlfriend, that Imogene had been doing it with her office assistant, Harriet, that Wally had had it with Imogene's not marrying him, that Imogene couldn't take Wally's leaving his keys in the porcelain bowl anymore, that Wally didn't care enough about Saks Fifth Avenue, that Imogene didn't care an iota about turtles, that Wally had found incriminating receipts in Imogene's pocket, that Imogene caught Wally taking laundry out of the dryer when the clothes had yet to dry thoroughly, that Wally felt Imogene harassed him about the clutter on his desk, that Imogene didn't like the way Wally pronounced the word *harass,* that Wally insisted on turning their dining alcove into a crafts center, that Imogene reclaimed the top drawer in the bureau, that Wally wanted to move to Buenos Aires, that Imogene was afraid of flying and refused to budge, that Wally had become a late-life gambler, that Imogene had obsessive-compulsive disorder, that Wally had been thrown in jail for selling the anesthetic ketamine, that things took a terrible turn for the worse when Wally found out that Imogene had changed her middle initial, that Imogene could never trust Wally after he'd confessed to jaywalking, that Wally was off his rocker and Imogene was a nutbird or was it the other way around, that it was the money thing, that moving from one domicile to another frequently results in turbulence (the Real Estate Theory of Divorce), that Wally and Imogene had religious differences though neither was religious, that they couldn't agree about what temperature to set the thermostat on, that they quarreled over the last slice of pizza until teeth were gnashed and tears were shed, that they walked at different velocities, that they were sick of each other's family, friends, and table manners, that they had different tastes in chewing gum and salad dressing, that they bickered bitterly about the best name for a dog though neither especially wanted a dog, and yes, the kid thing was broached. They said, well, it was one of those things, not meant to be, for the best, you win a few, you lose a few, no use crying over spilt milk, that's the way the cookie crumbles, tomorrow's another day.

405.

To Imogene, they said: So sorry, how are you holding up, call me anytime, nothing lasts, you did what you had to do, I would have done the same thing, there's no such thing as wrong, you're better off, it's not about you, give it time, what an asshole, men! I know a guy.

406.

Imogene scrubbed the ceilings in the apartment, and not just once.

407.

Imogene's friends were concerned. "You don't seem your-self," Harriet said to Imogene. The two were stapling satin flutter panties to mannequins.

"Who do I seem like?" said Imogene, looking fixedly at her assistant. Harriet froze.

"Medusa," thought Harriet. "Or Martin Balsam?" Did she mean Martin Buber?*

408.

Imogene did not believe in God, a fortunate thing because if His Tremendousness existed, Imogene was sure she'd be in big trouble. Imogene did, however, believe that if some-thing bad happened to her, then something good would follow. As a kid, hadn't she always been allowed to stay home from school and watch TV when she was sick? The system owed her, and the system had to pay up. As Imo-gene listened to Donald Charm's message asking her to call back right away, her heart fluttered.

---

*She meant Martin Bormann.

409.

"When one door closes, another opens, or something like that," Imogene thought. She hoped the something wasn't a tenth-story window.

410.

"Excuse the dotted Swiss," said Donald Charm, clearing an area on his sofa so that Imogene had a place to sit. The office was chockablock with ladies' attire and artwork featuring bulldogs. "Care for a biscuit?" said Donald Charm, holding out a large cookie jar shaped like a canine.

Imogene declined.

411.

Imogene was not crazy.

412.

But how could Imogene not be gladdened? According to Donald Charm, the low-cut Coquette in mauve was a runaway bestseller at Saks.

413.

"This is it!" Imogene thought.

414.

"This is the Moment," Imogene thought.

415.

"That said," said Mr. Charm, sticking a straight pin into a mini stuffed pooch, "I do not feel, after mulling it over, that Saks Fifth Avenue and Featherware make for a good fit." He cleared his throat and continued. "At this moment."

416.

Without so much as a stitch of mulling, Imogene took the contract in her hands and emended it into confetti.

417.

Just when things could get no worse, seven years went by. With age, Imogene's hair had turned redder. Wally still had the heart of a teenager. Probably pancreas, too.

418.

They ran into each other at the top of the Eiffel Tower. Isn't that funny, living in the same greater metropolitan area, and then meeting there? After all these years?

419.

Imogene was in town on a fashion shoot, and Wally had wanted to show the triplets La Ville Lumière, which, as he made them well aware, means the light city, not the city of lights. Wally's wife, Viva Leland, was a stay-at-home dentist.

To an observer, it looked as if Imogene and Wally were happy to intersect, but looks can be deceiving.

420.

"Are you still making soufflés?" Wally asked Imogene.

"Éclairs," said Imogene. "And oui."

421.

FINIS

422.

This is not the first time our book has screeched to a halt. Smart money might have it that it will not be the last. That's life for you. Everything ends, usually not soon enough and often with a criminal and civil lawsuit. But this is not life, and neither was that. Besides, everyone knows there is never an end of anything, just an ever-moving middle.

While you are attempting to reckon with the irreconcil-ability of this paradox (you know, the endless end), let us return to the ever-moving middle of ours. Specifically, let us return to the goings-on in chaplette 391.

423.

So when were we?

424.

5:03.

425.

5:03?
Excuse me.
The cookies are burning!

426.

Wallace Gilfeather-Yez, Jr., was pulled into the world after a horrendous thirty-nine-hour war. When Imogene held the newborn, she looked into his eyes and said, "Will I ever forgive you?"

427.

During visiting hours, Imogene fingered the hook-and-eye samples and pantaloon prototypes from her overnight bag as she briefed her assistant, Harriet, about various book-keeping tasks that would be of no interest to anyone else. Imogene said goodbye to Harriet, thanking her for the Kanga-Rocka-Roo, though she would have preferred a Vespa in Excalibur Gray. The baby slept like a baby.

428.

Another thing Wally Jr. did like a baby was scream. Imogene thought to call the fire department. Imogene's maternity leave lasted a little less than five minutes. Wally (Sr.), being Wally, gladly took two weeks off from work until Rosie from the nanny agency could take over.

429.

Time being time, Wallace Gilfeather-Yez, Jr., turned three. "What is your favorite animal?" his father said. "Is a dwarf an animal?" young Wally asked, and when he was told that it was not, he paused to reflect. "Then a cow," he said. Not far away, in the kitchen pantry, a puppy with a bow around its neck barked.

430.

A puppy, a toddler.

431.

Imogene insisted, no second baby. That thing they had, it was a baby, wasn't it?

432.

LinLin Gilfeather-Yez was born in Nanchang in the Jiangxi province of China. When Wally and Imogene introduced the baby to Wally Jr.—or Bounce, as the little boy was now called—he bit her on the neck.

433.

LinLin Gilfeather-Yez's first word was *ow*!

434.

This was her third word, too.

435.

And seventh.

436.

It was a fine start.

437.

As he did every night, Wally tiptoed into LinLin's room to ascertain that the child had not been kidnapped, murdered, or replaced with a Parchesi token, candlestick, round of Brie, or can of bug spray. On this night, however, just as Wally was exiting, LinLin startled Wally by opening her eyes wide and uttering her first word that was not an expression of pain.

Verging on the berserk, Wally scooped LinLin up and rushed her down the hall to Imogene, who was having a messy time dying fabric in the bathroom. "Say it again for Mommy," said Wally. "Come on, baby."

438.

"Whistleblower," said the twenty-seven-week-old.

439.

Could there have been a specimen more precocious? If only there were an Infant Olympics.

440.

One day Wally and Imogene watched in wonderment as LinLin grabbed a fresh diaper and, after a certain amount of writhing on the floor, successfully changed herself. Wally clapped heartily, snatched the baby up, and tossed her into the air friskily. "Immy, please," Wally said, the baby in his arms, "you've got to let me take her to the lab and put some electrodes on her. She's too good not to study."

441.

Imogene came home from work that night and before she could take off her coat, she announced to Wally that she wanted to throw in the towel, or rather, the undies. "Listen to this," she said, removing a newspaper clip from her pocket and reading. "A Mrs. DeeDee Doe was found in her home gym Thursday, dangling by the strap of her Featherware brassiere."

"It happens," said Wally, trying to be reassuring.

Imogene continued reading. "According to an anonymous lawyer, the estate plans to sue, charging the tragedy was the garment's fault." Imogene sighed. "It was from our Last Dance line. Why wasn't she wearing a sports bra?"

"On the bright side," said Wally, facetiously patting his midriff, "it's another reason not to exercise." He plopped into an armchair.

442.

The next day, there was a page-three story. They called it the Isadora Duncan bra.

443.

All news is not good news.

444.

The defense cited the safety record of underwear throughout history. The case was settled out of court. Featherware agreed that all products would henceforth come with a warning label.

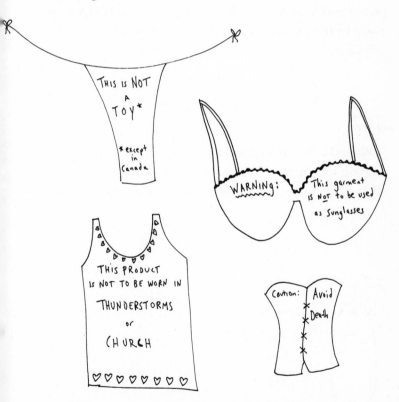

445.

In the marketplace, there are sellers and buyers, and Imogene said she was tired of being a seller. Did she want to be a buyer? Not really.

446.

The cost of private education in New York City has been well documented.* There is no need to rehash it in these pages. Needless to say, Wally and Imogene decided to move to the suburbs—there to await their midlife crises, they said.

447.

Wally and Imogene took out a mortgage to buy a house they didn't want. Inherited money would have come in handy. "Why is it," Imogene said, "that only poor people die?"

*

448.

shortcut

Mysterious odor

House with year-round Halloween decorations.

Rich People

Jews

Millard Fillmore supposedly drank a stein of ale and took a bath here.

• Wally and Imogene live here.

Location, location, location

WALLY AND IMOGENE'S NEW NEIGHBORHOOD

Intersection where Billy Pray was run over on his bike and three years later, his twin was killed by a drunk driver. The next week, their sister found a $20 bill on this spot.

You are here ↓.

449.

Not too long after the Gilfeather-Yez family was ensconced in their new house, Harriet stopped by with gifts for the children as well as a stack of business checks for Imogene to sign and a shopping bag of food because there is no food to speak of in the suburbs. Imogene had not seen Harriet for a while. Imogene could not remember the last time she had laid eyes on anyone who was not a relative, a UPS deliveryman, a medical professional, or an animated TV character. Imogene did her utmost to talk to Harriet in grown-up words, slipping up most egregiously after Imogene spilled a cup of coffee and exclaimed, "Whoops—I mean, fuck."

While the children and dog napped, Imogene showed Harriet every nook and cranny of the house. "This used to be the laundry room," Imogene said, "but does anyone really want to do laundry downstairs? So we were going to turn it into a kind of pantry, and then I thought, 'Pantry?' Why not knock down a wall—there was a wall here—and create a playroom by stealing some footage from the boiler room?"

450.

Harriet nodded.

451.

"You sure you don't want anything else to eat, Harr?" said Imogene.

"Actually," said Harriet, "do you think if I leave now, I could make the five fifty-eight?"

"Don't you want to see the crawl space?" said Imogene, opening the door to the basement. Harriet looked at her watch. "When Wally comes home," said Imogene, "he can drive you to the station."

"It's just that I told Lawrence—" said Harriet, not finishing the sentence.

452.

Imogene had no choice. She offered Harriet a share of the business—first 15 percent, and then when it looked as if she could still make the five fifty-eight, 25 percent. "Thanks for sharing," Harriet said with a hint of wryness.

453.

Harriet stayed for dinner. It was just the two of them at the table because Wally was not yet home from work, and the children were not mature enough for the dining room. Later, after Imogene put Bounce and LinLin to bed, Harriet made her escape. "You are so lucky," Harriet said to her new business partner as Imogene opened the front door.

454.

Whoever sees Imogene cry? Even Patty hasn't. Imogene was weeping up a storm when Wally returned home from work. She had been done in by Bounce's Big Boy Racing Car bed. The footboard grille had come off, and then one of the hubcap-and-wheel assemblies. While Bounce was having a tantrum, Imogene did what she could to repair the wreck, but then the chassis lay collapsed on the floor like a capsized boat. LinLin had a go at putting the bed back together, but a baby can do only so much, even if she's LinLin.

There would be no rest today.

455.

There would be much talk of nap schedules.

456.

"This is not how I expected it," Imogene whimpered.

457.

Wally knew what she meant.

458.

It hadn't turned out the way Wally imagined either. Wally had trusted that they would have figured out deep solar power, that money wouldn't matter, and that peanut butter cookies would taste as good as they looked on the box. Aside from that, Wally was jubilant beyond his most optimistic dreams. The world had delivered and then some. This view was something he was keeping to himself right now. Instead, he quickly and quietly reassembled the bed. "Immy, you did all the work," said Wally, putting his hand on Imogene's head. "I just stepped in and added the finishing touch."

(That night, the moon was low and full, and emanating from the orb, a faint lunar bow could be seen, a rare occurrence, for sure.)

459.

Imogene had read studies about what happens to children whose mothers work full-time. The prognosis was dire. Depression, drugs, suicide, astigmatism, embezzlement, assassination, bankruptcy, alien abduction, asbestosis, ingrown nails, phantom limbs, ingrown toenails on phantom limbs, lice, moths, split ends, scrofula. Bounce, she figured, was iffy enough already. Lately, the child had been going off to the houses of playmates and bringing home their toilet plungers.

460.

You could call it stealing.

461.

Bounce called it getting even.

462.

Imogene knew "rationally" that she could not "have" everything, but just as "rationally," she did not see why not. She called Harriet and asked for her desk back. Not asked. Demanded. It was Imogene's desk.

463.

Ah, the grown-up world of baby dolls, teddies, and boy shorts. Not to mention latex shapewear.

464.

There were still the weekends.

465.

One Saturday morning, circa dawn, Imogene stubbed her toe on a plastic brontosaurus that should have been else-where. "Do you think it's broken?" she said, limping over to Wally, who'd just finished reading aloud a book about big trucks and little trucks. She meant her toe, not the toy, which was indestructible, having already been run over by a big car and a little car and put through the wash. "Even if it is," Wally said, "there's nothing medical science can do about it."

466.

Imogene flopped onto the floor, a lamentation on the limitation of medical science for which Wally was partly responsible.

467.

"Do you remember when we were above this?" said Imogene.

468.

"I remember when you thought we were," Wally said.

469.

"Actually," Wally said, "I remember when we thought we were."

470.

But that's not what he meant.

471.

The Gilfeather-Yez family was no stranger to the ER. There had been tree house disasters, dives down laundry chutes, so-called accidents with spoons, and unfortunate outcomes of a game called Dead Girl. Last week, it was Bounce's turn. He'd been taken by his parents to the hospital, screaming that he'd finessed one of LinLin's princess beads into his nose, ever to remain there, it seemed. "You will feel a slight discomfort, and then it will be over," said the doctor, who had a light on his head. Did he say this to Bounce or to Wally and Imogene? In either case, after the doctor removed the bead, Bounce screamed that the bead in question had been yellow.

472.

Not blue.

473.

The next day, LinLin, for her part, suffered an occupational injury while serving as the target for her brother's target practice. That was a sort of coup de grace.

474.

A lady from Social Services visited the house.

475.

"We can explain," said Imogene.

476.

The lady didn't seem to hear, for she was on her way to the basement, presumably looking for the nunchuck.

477.

"Do you have electric toothbrushes on the premises?" the Social Services lady asked.

478.

Was this a trick question?

479.

Wally said yes.

480.

Imogene said no.

481.

A report was filed.

482.

A man from Social Services called Wally to tell him that he and his wife had been put on probation. "Probation?" said Wally.

483.

The next morning, Bounce, perhaps sensing a power shift, firmly stated he would not eat his Count Chocula unless he could have Clamato in the bowl.

484.

Imogene thought twice before she told her son to shut up and eat.

485.

The urgency with which Imogene begged Wally, and not just once, to take out a life insurance policy made Wally question whether she knew something about his health that he did not. Or was she planning to do him in? Eight million dollars is a lot of money. Indeed, when Wally's flight to Dallas–Fort Worth touched down safely, he felt a twinge of disappointment.

486.

Besides, ultimately, who's a survivor?

(There were areas of patchy fog along the coast, with visibility of only a few feet. Fortunately, nobody wanted to see farther.)

487.

Bounce was too old to wet his bed, but nevertheless, nearly every night, he managed to defeat the odds.

488.

The boy was taken to a child psychologist who observed Bounce playing with blocks before delivering the verdict.

489.

"The kid's a lazy good-for-nothing, and will never get into a good college."

490.

"Where did we go wrong?" said Imogene on the drive home. "Oh, Wal!" she moaned. "Should we get him a blocks tutor?"

491.

"I was thinking that if I had to do it all over again," Wally said, "I might become a polymer chemist."

492.

LinLin was perfect. She never cried, ate with gusto, went to sleep soon after being put to bed, and took an interest in books, if tearing them up can be called an interest. On her first day of day care, LinLin did not fuss when Imogene said goodbye. The other parents were envious. When Imogene returned home, she telephoned Wally in some distress. "I read that when nothing seems wrong, it's a sign of something really wrong," she said.

493.

"She's only in the sixty-second percentile for height," Wally reassured Imogene.

494.

then the tV brakes and dady sed I
can ficks it if the babee gets
Out uf the houtz. NOw!

495.

According to Jean-Jacques Rousseau, the political philoso-
pher, not the wholesale egg distributor from Indianapolis,
unadulterated happiness can be had through contemplation
so profound that the contemplator enters into a state where
time seems to stand still. Imogene and Wally didn't need
Rousseau to tell them why they weren't happy.

(Funtime Factoid: Jean-Jacques Rousseau had five children. He abandoned them to a foundling institution.)

496.

Wally and Imogene bickered about who would stay home and who would go to preschool parent orientation, though which was preferable was clear to neither. On the domestic front, you were sure to face disaster. In the Groves of Academe, you, along with three real estate agents, two jewelry designers, one therapist, five stay-at-home moms, one sad widow, and one wholesale purveyor of kosher brisket, would sit at little desks, listening to Miss Scattergood hold forth on which days there will be juice with the cookies (no raisins!) and why we must wash our hands after we go to the toilet.

"I gotta get out of here," thought Imogene. "I gotta get out of here," thought Wally.

497.

So yes, there were times that Imogene and Wally thought alike.

498.

Oliver, a boy in Bounce's class, died while doing his homework. The next day, the children in grades one through four were allowed fifteen minutes extra recess time. They were also invited, though not required, to sign the "Deepest Sympathies" poster that Principal Rakoff had handmade for the occasion.

499.

To Oliver's parents, Bounce wrote, "Maybeee hes not dead! ☺ ."

500.

Other children LinLin's age had probably never even heard the word, but LinLin was advanced. She was able to use the word *liquidator* in a fully formed sentence. "Promise not to laugh at me," LinLin said to Imogene and Wally one night as they put her to bed, "but I think I might be a liquidator." The girl sat bolt upright to present her case. No matter how hard she tried, Imogene could not conceal her alarm.

501.

Outside LinLin's room, Imogene whispered to Wally, "Should we take her to a psychiatrist?"

"Let her be," said Wally, observing their daughter, who was fast asleep, despite the awkward arrangement of her limbs. Unbeknownst to her parents, LinLin had assiduously trained herself to sleep this way, believing the position to be the one she'd least likely mind being frozen in forever if, God forbid, she were stricken by something gruesome in the middle of the night. "See how happy she looks," said Wally.

"But, Wal," said Imogene.

"Besides," said Wally, "how do we know she really isn't a liquidator?"

502.

Sooner or later, thought Imogene, there was bound to be trouble.

503.

Imogene waited for something to go wrong, but so far Lin-Lin remained preternaturally okay. She had an abundance of friends, was a favorite of teachers, babysitters, and food deliverymen, and when she was in the first grade, her classmates voted her Most Likely to Succeed in Second Grade. LinLin's persistent lack of problems irked Imogene no end.

"Let's get this over with," Imogene thought.

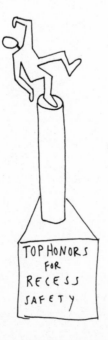

TOP HONORS
FOR
RECESS
SAFETY

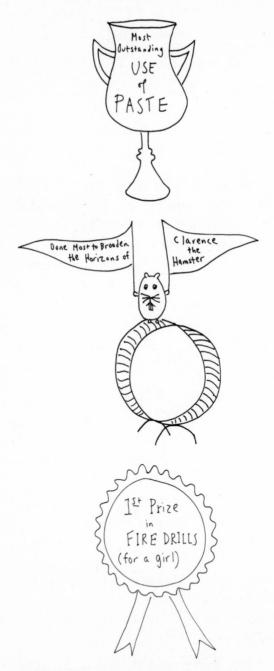

504.

She was so anxious that one day Imogene paid a visit to Dr. Kleaner. "Can I tell you something?" she said to the doctor. "Never have children."

"Yes," said Dr. Kleaner, nodding.

"Are some infinities not more infinite than others?" said Imogene.

Dr. Kleaner prescribed drugs for LinLin and Imogene, and some for himself, too.

Imogene was almost out the door when Dr. Kleaner said, "Knock, knock."

505.

A GUIDE TO PASTA SHAPES
BOUNCE WILL AND WILL NOT EAT

<u>Likes:</u>

Wagon
Wheels

Bow
Ties

Seashells

Macaroni
(with cream cheese)

<u>Dislikes:</u>

Fusilli
(especially green)

Spaghettini

Angel
Hair

Lasagna

K B Z
A D S P
   N O
Alphabet
(except "L")

<u>Willing to Take One Bite of:</u>

Rigatoni
(if you say it's
fettucini)

Bucatini
(after
inspection)

Penne
(on Tuesdays)

gramigna
(if boiled sixteen
hours)

Must Be Covered With a Dishtowel:

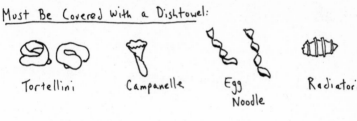

Tortellini   Campanelle   Egg Noodle   Radiatori

Cannot Be In Same Room As:

Orecchiette   Creste di galli   Fiore   Ravioli

Loves, but only for Throwing Purposes:

gnocchi   Orzo   Vermicelli   Racchiate

506.

To the readers who have felt themselves swept with consternation regarding the brevity of the chaplettes, Patty asks, "Have you checked out life lately?"

507.

Life too short? "Not short enough," thought Wally. Wally was in his lab at Weenix Corp., waiting, for scientific reasons, for yet another chipmunk to digest yet another nut.

508.

Wally's Chipmunk Log, page 183

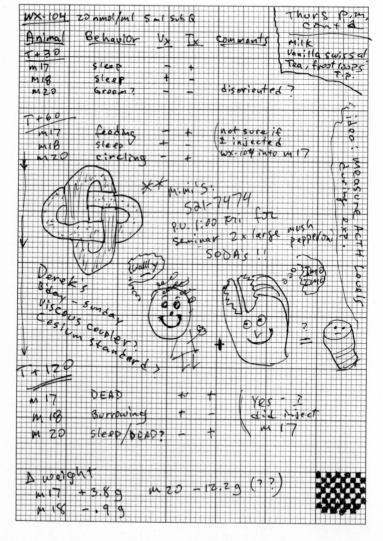

509.

The Homework Years.

510.

It was a time of uncertainty, bloodshed, strife, brother against sister, mother against father, uneaten spinach, fractions.

511.

"Mom, do you like my collar this way . . ." Bounce stood still so his witness could behold, and then when he felt enough beholding had taken place, he said, "Or this way?"

512.

To the beholder, the collar was the same. To the boy in love with the girl who did not know his name, it had been slightly but meaningfully angled.

513.

"Uh, the second way, Bouncy," said Imogene, who was preoccupied trying to think of the word that was like ethnic cleansing but not exactly.

514.

"You sure?" said Bounce, turning to look at himself in the mirror. "You don't think my hair makes me look like a horse, do you? I want to look like that president person, Andrew Jackson."

515.

"Genocide!"

516.

At the Sepkowitz dinner party, Imogene sat next to a psychoanalyst who told her that becoming a parent was an enriching experience.

"Richer with what exactly?" asked Imogene.

The doctor did not or perhaps would not reply. He intently pushed his food into neat little nontouching piles. Anyway, the answer wasn't money.

What about Imogene's other dining companion? The man was an engineer at the Department of Transportation, where he mapped traffic patterns on bridges. He was on sabbatical, he told Imogene, so that he could volunteer at the local high school, reorganizing their trophy case.

Imogene contemplated the activity at the other end of the table. The guests were laughing and yakking down there, listening raptly and listening mirthfully. "Look at them," Imogene thought, "exchanging blithe repartée, flirting gamesomely, forging friendships, making business deals, divulging insider information, confiding sublime tidbits of gossip, spilling the beans, telling all, recounting stories that would knock your socks off." Why was it, Imogene wondered, that the really great stuff always happened at the other end of the table?

517.

Why was it that it was always a French dinner party over there?

518.

Wally was sitting in the nucleus of merriment. To his side sat a former rock-and-roll star and model who had just been appointed Minister of Culture of an African country. On Wally's other side was Jesus Christ.

519.

Next to Imogene, the psychoanalyst was quarantining carrots and making pariahs of his potatoes Diane.

520.

Wouldn't you know it? At the next Sepkowitz dinner party, Imogene was seated next to a man who manufactured parts for machines that made manufacturing parts. He had seemed depressed, Imogene told Wally post-party. Wally thought the man looked undepressed.

Imogene shook her head. "Anyone who buys a summer house in Nebraska is depressed," she said.

"Nebraska, the crimes-against-humanity place?" said Wally.

"Uh-hunh," said Imogene.

"Interesting," said Wally.

521.

Life tries hard to bring us down, but it faced a dogged athlete when it fucked with Wally.

522.

That night, at what promised to be the apex of the act, Imogene yawned. Wally did not notice. According to magazines one reads in line at the supermarket, these things happen all the time.

523.

Later, while Wally slept, Imogene calculated the number of miles she had racked up carpooling the children. Had she driven in a straight line, and had her car been an amphibious vehicle, she figured that she'd have crossed the Pyrenees by now.

524.

Patty has never been to the Pyrenees, but she has been to Upper Darby, Pennsylvania. Also to hell and back.*

---

* Total mileage: 13,435,637. Rest stops along route: 1. Best souvenir: limbo dishtowel.

RAPHY ACCORDING
TO BOUNCE
St. Louis is a lake
Northwest Passage
Iceland
Old York
Frisbeeville
Holy Roman Empire
Not as little as it looks
New York
Deep dish pizza
ia
Upper Something
Above the Fruited Plain
Lower Something
Fruited Plain
Our Ocean
Miami
Your ami
Eerie Canal
se
diana
The Carrot Being

525.

(Quarter-size hail changing to half-dollar size fell over all of northern South Dakota, leaving dozens without power. Southern North Dakota was so glad it gloated.)

526.

Missy Winkelman called Imogene to say she knew it was short notice but she was canceling Thanksgiving. If the phone had rung just a few minutes later, Imogene's parsnip puree and shaved Brussels sprout casserole would have been soundly wrapped in foil, and the Gilfeather-Yez family would have been on their way to the Winkelmans'.

"Looks like we'll just have to stay home and watch the game, right, Dad?" said Bounce when he heard the news.

"You know, it's against the law to call off a national holiday," said LinLin when she heard the news.

"Why do you always have to be so anti-illegal?" said Bounce, taking off his jacket and throwing it at his sister.

"Mom," said LinLin.

"Okay, that's enough," said Imogene.

527.

Talk about your understatements!

528.

When the kids were upstairs, Imogene whispered, "How-ie's having an affair with a twenty-four-year-old dance therapist."

Wally ruminated on the news. Finally, he said: "I think I know which one."

"It's a shame for Missy," said Imogene, "but if we're forced to pick sides, let's go with Howie. He has a lawn mower."

529.

Howie? Who's Howie? Patty knows a Hal, Howard, Hubert, and Bob, but no Howie. Truth be told, Imogene's yet to meet Howie, and if I know Patty, probaby won't.

530.

Wally and Imogene were in the basement, arguing about the boiler, when Bounce appeared on the stairs. He wanted to talk about something, he said, and it couldn't wait. "I hope you know that we would love you just as much if you were gay," Wally said, adding, "maybe even more." Bounce rolled his eyes.

"Let's not go overboard," thought Imogene.

531.

"From now on," Bounce said, "my name is Irving."

(The Irving phase was short-lived, but not as short-lived as the Floyd phase. By the end of the week, Wallace Gilbert Gilfeather-Yez, Jr., was Bounce once again, and will remain so for the remainder of the book.)

532.

Being in a relationship, Imogene had come to see, meant figuring out new ways to phrase "I told you so."

533.

Wally's co-worker poked his head into the lab. "Someone is here to see you, and it's urgent," he said. Wally threw a pellet onto some cedar shavings.

"I take it you're up on the Frazier findings in this month's *Aging Cell*?" Wally heard someone say. He didn't have to turn around to know who it was. Gwen always knew a tad more than Wally, sometimes even a tad and a half.

Wally regarded Gwen. Could this be the same woman he had shared so many dual museum memberships with? How many years, Wally tried to remember, had it been since Gwen had left him for Leonard?

Is that what Gwen had done? Is that how it happened?

534.

Patty must be on record somewhere saying there is never any way of knowing who was the jilter, who the jiltee.

535.

No matter. Wally beheld Gwen with fondness, sympathy, nostalgia, sadness, goodwill.

536.

Plus lust.

537.

Wally liked her blouse.

538.

"How's Tran?" Wally said.

539.

"Trench," said Gwen. "He was suspended from middle school for embezzlement."

"Kids," said Wally, because what else could anyone say?

540.

Not the correct response: *"They grow up so fast, don't they? One minute, you're changing a diaper, the next you're posting bail for moping with intent to loiter."*

541.

"I'm here for a reason," said Gwen. Wally sensed doom. Reasons were rarely reasons, Wally thought. Gwen reached into her tote bag and brought out a cookie tin. She wasn't planning to poison him with Norwegian butter cookies, was she? She took the lid off the cookies, revealing a pasty white sandy powder.

"Holy shit!" said Wally, doing the blinking version of a double take.

"Don't get your hopes up," said Gwen. "It's Stuffy. He never came out of hibernation." She grabbed a beaker off a shelf. "How about I put your half of the cremains in this?" Gwen said, visibly unencumbered by any of the stages of grief, with the possible exception of anger and greed. "Your half of the vet bill's in the mail," Gwen said as she poured. Wally no longer esteemed the blouse.

542.

He still had respect for her tits, though.

543.

Home from work, Wally kissed Imogene hello and squeezed her shirt. "On the radio just now they said couples who make each other laugh and don't fight live longer," Wally said.

544.

Imogene pondered the news. "Not worth it," she said.

545.

Patty has taken to bed.

546.

She's up. Whew! That was a close call.

547.

An e-mail whose subject line was "High Priority" awaited Wally when he arrived at work. Wally had higher priorities. He stopped by the cafeteria for a chocolate chip muffin, tried to figure out, with a colleague, who was also getting a muffin, how long it would take them to build a dam across the creek near the lab, did the crossword puzzle, asked around to see if anyone had a mint, stared at the chipmunks, cracked his knuckles, touched his toes, and took a nap. He was woken up by a memo, sung to him with vibrato by his lab mate, who had an upcoming audition at the amateur opera troupe in Guttesdumberg, Tennessee. The memo was from the senior scientist at Weenix, directing the development team, of which Wally was a member, to commence clinical trials straightaway on the company's antinausea drug, code-named Ephron.

Do actual work at his job? You must be kidding.

548.

Maybe, thought Wally, it was time to bid adieu to nausea and find another calling. He cooked last meals for the lab subjects whose lives were to end the next day. Cooked? More like took wrappers off the Snickers bars and Reese's Peanut Butter Cups.

549.

Wally's options: Study petrography. Become a compass-smith.* Found an origami museum made out of spelt paper. Open a newsstand that carries only magazines from the week before. Visit every state in alphabetical order. Lose the paunch. Learn how to levitate. Take Bounce and Lin-Lin on a trip they'll never forget. Clone Stuffy. Figure out

---

Compasssmith is one of the few non-ridiculous words to have three successive *s*'s.

a way to get in touch with Beenish Asif. Cure eczema. Go to the dentist. Don't go to the dentist.

Wally was becoming increasingly chipper about what lay ahead until what lay ahead was really lying there.

550.

Wally remained at Weenix. Whatever the drawbacks, he, no longer a kid, had to be realistic: the muffins in the cafeteria were first-rate and he had a parking space.

551.

"I'd like to say that this is the result of a trauma," said the doctor, shaking his head as he looked over Wally's X-rays. Wally had come to the doctor to get a flu shot.

"But I'm not going to lie to you, Wally," the doctor continued. He cleared his throat, and recommended that Wally see another doctor.

552.

Imogene slipped on the ice outside the supermarket. Though she did not suffer an injury or even feel pain, Imogene turned sad and sentimental. She wondered if this would be the last time she would ever fall without breaking something. Meanwhile, Bounce sprained his ankle trying to fracture someone's ankle, and LinLin won the spelling bee on account of the word *cartilage*.

553.

552 was the osteo-chaplette of the Gilfeather-Yez family.

554.

Did anything go well for Wally and Imogene in these years? Were there moments of happiness? Sure there were, but is that the kind of book you want to read?

555.

On the other hand, Fernanda Kimball's *Kiki Loses a Tooth but Gains a Best Friend* is on Patty's bedside table.

FRESH AIR & HOW TO USE IT

Let's Make Some Undies!

HOW TO WRITE

Celebrating Cardboard Boxes

SCIENCE EXPLAINED

What's Wrong With the Huguenots

7 ESSENTIAL BOOKS for your BEDSIDE

556.

Wally tried the carrot and Imogene tried the stick, but neither got anywhere. Bounce refused to come out of his room and say hello to their dinner guests, and that was that. These days, Bounce hardly ever came out of his room, or so it seemed to his parents, who failed to realize how good they had it. LinLin, of course, always captured the hearts and minds of dinner guests. She played a tuba sonata she'd composed, and chatted enthusiastically about Renaissance poetry, German board games, botanical printmaking, and competitive duck-herding.

557.

"Bounce is studying," Imogene would finally say to her guests. "It's mortifying," she would have to say to Wally later when they were cleaning up.

"Oh, Im, let 'im be," said Wally, idly gazing.

"Do you think he'll become a felon?" said Imogene.

"I can think of worse things," said Wally.

558.

Imogene froze. Worse?

559.

Imogene was reluctant to leave Bounce alone in the house for the weekend, especially since he said he'd given them his word that he was going to spend the whole time writing his report on the economic future of Paraguay and maybe even compare it to Uruguay if his parents would just stay out of his hair for just one day more. "Don't you trust me?" were Bounce's parting words to Imogene and Wally before they pulled out of the driveway with LinLin.

It was a question that answered itself.

560.

Imogene and Wally were taking LinLin to tuba and euphonium camp in Ohio.

561.

At the police station, Bounce said, "It wasn't my fault." The list of wrongdoers was long, and Bounce had only gotten up to implicating Steve Stringfield when an officer whisked him away to Mug Shots and Fingerprints.

WALLY YEZ, JR. : INDEX, LEFT

562.

"Don't you think we should punish him?" said Imogene.

563.

"How can anyone punish a kid who has a lawyer?" said Wally.

564.

What crime had Bounce committed or, as his defense contends, not committed? He and his posse, fueled by booze and foodstuffs from the Gilfeather-Yez pantry, had outlined a twenty-foot picture in the snow on the lawn of Leftie's Funeral Home. The image is too lewd to represent in this book, but Patty offers this substitute:

565.

Poor Imogene had broken out in hives. Her condition had an etiology that stemmed from an allergy she'd developed to wearing clothes made before 1986, even madras. The '60s go-go dress went bye-bye. As did the op art hot pants, the spandex jump suit, and the floral print granny dress. All donated to charity.

566.

It was an international tragedy.

567.

On the ride home from the precinct, Imogene closed her eyes. They passed the house with the crazy shrubbery and the intersection where everyone had the right of way. "Wal," she said, opening her eyes when they reached the spot where Davey Weiner maimed his father in the elbow with a BB gun, "Bounce is going to have a mark on his permanent record."

"It's okay, Im," said Wally, reassuringly putting his non-steering hand on hers. "We all do." Wally had no idea what he was talking about.

"Do you know anyone who can alter a permanent record?" said Imogene.

Wally did, but unfortunately, Sergeant Timothy, Elsie's brother, was on some kind of nutty scruples kick.

568.

To lull herself to sleep, Imogene lay in bed, counting her divorced friends. She was up to twenty-seven, but then she deducted one because, technically, Harriet was only angry at the asshole.

Imogene was trying to get to number forty-four when Wally slipped into the bedroom, home late again for the umpteenth time in whenever. He kicked off his shoes and leaned over to kiss Imogene on the forehead. Imogene did not stir. She was considering whether she would ever leave Wally.

569.

At least once a day that fall, Imogene or Wally would ask Bounce, in the most deferential way, if he'd filled out his college applications yet. Bounce's reply always went something along the lines of "If they don't want me for who I am inside, then give me one good reason I should go to their shithole college."

"A car," said Imogene. "We'll buy you a car."

"If I don't go to college, I don't need a car," said Bounce, as if he were coming up with a helpful solution. "I'll use your car."

"A speedboat?" said Imogene.

"How about if we all fill them out together?" said Wally. "We can order Chinese."

570.

One night, without being prodded, Bounce completed his application to the only college to which he intended to apply. The essay question was: "Creative people often state that taking risks often promotes important discoveries which oftenly occur in their personal or intellectual life. In your opinion, what is the greatest risk you ever took?"

Bounce's essay consisted of the following two words:

"Up yours."

571.

The day would come and the day did come when the impeccable LinLin at last gave her mother grief. LinLin, though only a college junior, came home for the winter holidays with a diamond ring. "Maybe you should keep it in the box," Imogene said when LinLin showed her parents the surprise.

"Oh, Mom," said LinLin.

572.

LinLin's betrothed, Igor Flatev, had come to this country from Russia when he was ten, fleeing the oppression of the state and his parents. Iggy had made his way to Minnesota, where he convinced the first Slavic lady he ran into that he was her third cousin twice removed. She and her husband took the immigrant in, and raised him as if he were their son, with one exception: Iggy was required to take out the garbage.

573.

Iggy did as he was told—and told Wally and Imogene of his suffering.

574.

LinLin wrote a poem featuring Iggy's suffering. Nonrhyming—"but only in a literal sense," she said.

575.

> *Garbage in, garbage out.*
> *Tell me if you find my lost . . .** *

576.

Imogene was not inclined to be positive about what would likely ensue. "She's not even twenty," Imogene said to Wally in the kitchen one night as they were cleaning up after dinner.

"Just because you don't want to get married," said Wally, "doesn't mean the world can't. Where does salt go?" Wally looked around, and then, taking a gamble, put the salt shaker in the cabinet with the cereal.

---

*Here the poem breaks off. LinLin had been reading *Dead Souls* at the time, a novel that ends in mid-sentence because the author, Nikolai Gogol, burned the rest of his manuscript and subsequently went mad and died. This impressed LinLin greatly.

"Why can't she get into something reasonable?" said Imogene, sorting the silverware. "Like kleptomania." She handed Wally the steak knives, pointing to the cutlery drawer.

577.

"Or sadism."

578.

Poor LinLin. It wasn't long before Igor Flatev left her for an etiquette coach.

578.2

How impolite.

579.

Hadn't Imogene shown sufficient sympathy? She thought so. Wally had a different opinion. "When your daughter calls to say that she's just been dumped by her fiancé," Wally said, perching himself on the edge of the bed, "can't you think of something to say besides 'He smelled like canned beets'?"

580.

Bounce was off seeing the world. He'd seen it before.

581.

In the Virgin Islands, of all places, Bounce met a virgin from the Principality of Andorra. Her English was spotty, but so was Bounce's. They had Not Communicating in common. The young woman's name was Uxue, which in English means nothing.

Uxue had ended up living in the Virgin Islands owing to an airline mix-up. At the airport, on her way from Andorra to Portugal to study gemology, Uxue had volunteered to give up her seat on an overbooked flight in return for a ticket on a later plane and a voucher for a moist towelette. She did not object when she learned that the later flight was headed somewhere she had not planned to go. Ever.

582.

A pouty-lipped brunette with a bone structure unequaled among the higher primates and a dimple in the right place, Uxue is, hands down, the best-looking character in this book.

583.

No character herein would dare claim otherwise, except maybe Gwen Dworkin.

584.

Gwen has issues.

585.

Not long after Bounce met X, as he affectionately called her, they were "doing it" night and day.

586.

What a difference a few years and good sense make. This time, when Imogene learned that one of her children was engaged, she showed her true colors and continued turning the pages of a magazine. It was not that Imogene had changed her mind about holy matrimony, but with LinLin it had been different. Imogene had had high hopes for Lin-Lin, whereas Bounce . . .

587.

Also, LinLin had been younger. To be sure, everyone had.

588.

"Nice," Imogene said to Bounce when he called from a beach in the Caribbean with the big news. Imogene returned to "The Revolution of Mascara."

Wally beamed as he listened in on the speakerphone. "How about that?" Wally said.

"Yeah," said Imogene. "That's pretty great."

"Um," said Bounce over the phone. Then Bounce said "um" again.

589.

There was a commotion on the other end of the line.

"Hello there, ancestors," said Uxue. "Like I much, um, sooner, wow!"

"I may have some ideas about the caterer," said Imogene. "But I don't know who eats these days."

After everyone had hung up, Wally said, "Well, she seemed terrific."

"Wal," said Imogene, "you think she sounded pregnant?"

590.

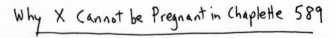

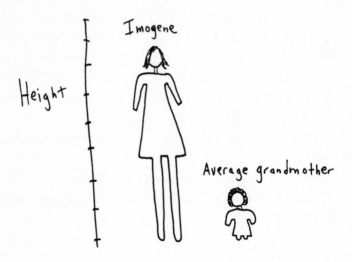

591.

In Terminal B, Imogene and Wally collected the happy couple. Bounce was the only passenger in baggage claim who had no baggage. Amended: Bounce had a fiancée who came with loads of lavish baggage. "Where's your toothbrush?" Imogene said to her son after she gave him a hug, unrumpled his jacket, and assessed his beard.

"Thailand?" said Bounce.

592.

Relating to grown-up children can be awkward and make you feel old. The parent must disguise her feelings of disappointment, resist the urge to carp, and figure out what words to say to this person who went away as flesh and blood, full of promise, and came back a disgusting stranger, more or less your age.

593.

"So," said Imogene, sitting across from Bounce and X in the living room, "they must have delicious pineapple in the Virgin Islands."

Wally appeared with an armful of leather-bound volumes. "Who wants to see photos of the best boy in history?" Bounce's da-da said buoyantly.

594.

No more pretending it'll all turn out okay.

595.

Much is made, symbolically speaking, of the significance of weather—not just by poets but also by creators of decorative pillows and by wedding toast-makers, for whom atmospheric conditions are to the future as Ouija boards are to the past. Today was no exception. "And so, let us raise our glasses," said Bounce's best man, "to a couple whose life together will be a mix of sun and clouds, which will give way to mainly clear skies in the late afternoon and a high of eighty-two."

596.

We cannot speak of what happened to Bounce and X in their eighties, for that interval is beyond the scope of this tome—indeed, this tome is beyond the scope of this tome. We can, however, say that this day was a happy day, in spite of anthrax and boils.

597.

Everyone was there, aside from Elsie, who later said she'd never received an invitation, and of course, Ron de Jean.

598.

"Im," said Wally, after the guests had left and the happy hosts were picking up cashew crumbs on the rug, "now that the kids are gone and it's just the two of us, won't you say yes?"

599.

"You're kidding," Imogene said.

600.

Imogene would have hesitated, but Patty put her (Imogene and Patty's) foot down just like that.

601.

Imogene was filing tax returns when her mother's house-keeper called. Erna Gilfeather had died in her sleep of something icky. Too suffused with ick to repeat here.

602.

"You're kidding," Imogene said to the housekeeper.
  Is everything a joke to Imogene?

603.

Yes. You bet. Why not?

604.

"Your mother was a fighter," said the housekeeper. The housekeeper said that Erna Gilfeather's last coherent words were: "Not yet. Not until I've worn the new clothes in my closet."

605.

The housekeeper sighed. "Your mother is in a better place," she said, "I mean, where she doesn't have to worry anymore about dying."

606.

Imogene stared at the IRS forms on her desk. She had expected her mother to live well into chaplette 609, maybe even eke it out till 610, if you could call literature a life.

607.

Imogene was trying to sleep, counting the grandchildren in her circle who'd been rejected from the nursery school of "their" choice. She felt certain she could get up to seven, but surprised herself by reaching nineteen.

608.

Could she think of the names of fifty-two candy bars? It was worth a try.

609.

But her heart wasn't in the game. What was so bad about staying awake, anyway?

610.

Imogene recollected the last time she'd seen her mother. Just months ago, they'd taken advantage of the Arbor Day sales to go shopping for bath mats. "Don't take this the wrong way, Immy," Mrs. Gilfeather had said as they waited for the sales associate to find a terrycloth oval in ecru (not cream!), "but were your eyebrows always asymmetrical?"

Imogene had turned and directed onto her mother a juvenile pout. "If I don't tell you the truth, who will?" Mrs. Gilfeather said.

Remembering this now, Imogene thought, "Good question."*

---

*The truth question, not the eyebrows one. Everyone's eyebrows are asymmetrical.

611.

Imogene got up early and shuffled into the bathroom. She turned on the dimmer light to minimum dim, and took her chances with the mirror. "You again," Imogene said into the bevel-edged oval she'd picked up in Venice long before she'd known Wally, even before she knew Ron de Jean. Whom had she gone to Venice with? She could not remember a name, or even a face. She could remember telephone numbers, though.

As Imogene searched for the correct emollient in the medicine cabinet, the door opened and Wally edged into the room. "Want to hear something?" he said with bright eyes.

"I already know," said Imogene.

"I'm in the mood for mocha mousse," said Wally.

"It's going to be an easy transition into senility," thought Imogene.

612.

At a garden party held in celebration of the Sepkowitzes' thirty-fifth wedding anniversary, Imogene and Wally were sipping cocktails by a splotch of pachysandra while, nearby, a bunch of men argued about which of them had the worst heart.

"Angioplasty?" said a smirking bottling plant magnate. "Brushing your teeth is more invasive. I had an angioplasty *with* a stent, and *then* they did a triple bypass."

"Quadruple," said a rock-and-roll one-hit wonder, tapping his chest vigorously. "Ripped out the veins from my legs and attached them to my coronary arteries."

"Pff, I'm on my second heart transplant," said a professor of human resources. "Legally, I'm seven-eighths dead."

A woman nobody knew approached the group. "Gentlemen," she said, "I had a leaky valve before any of you could tell your left nut from your right. Ebstein's anomaly, and it's congenital." The woman bid the men adieu, her stilettos sinking into the pachysandra bed as she departed.

Imogene took Wally's arm. "Let's get out of here," she said. "Our hearts are fine."

613.

Wally was still sleeping. He was dreaming that he was sleeping.

When he woke, not in the dream but from the dream, he was so tired, he decided to go back to sleep and pick up in the dream where he left off. But, whoa, did Wally forget about a little thing called time? Reentering REM, Wally dreamed he'd already shaved and showered and was downstairs eating a muffin for breakfast. That morning in real life, Wally, who had had a muffin for breakfast for the last twenty-seven years, went for the cereal. "Why aren't you having a muffin?" said Imogene.

"To show them," said Wally.

614.

This raises an interesting ontological question.

615.

What is an ontological question?

616.

The sum of the collective ages in years of the characters, named and unnamed, at this chaplette in time is 3,769.

617.

Imogene was at her desk, sorting through the mail in what used to be LinLin's room, and even now was painted in teenage vermilion. Perfect LinLin was off in Africa, being a pediatric hematologist. Wally poked his head in the door to ask whether Imogene had seen his reading glasses and also he was wondering who the love of her life was. "Who's yours?" she said.

618.

Imogene did not say so, but it unsettled her to acknowledge that she did not have a love of her life. "Want to order in tonight?" Imogene said.

(There was no weather that day. The world was room temperature.)

WALLACE YEZ, STABILITY SCIENTIST, FOUND DEAD

Wallace Yez, a neurobiologist whose work in dizziness led to breakthroughs in balance theory (though some put it conversely), died Thursday of natural causes in front of his refrigerator. He was ninety-two.

Yez was perhaps best known for the experiments he conducted at the Futter-Cohan Institute, in which he dropped herring from great heights. "He got a lot of criticism for that study," said Dr. Sammy Sokolow, a colleague, "but, ultimately, the work helped a lot of fish and led to the development of the Wall-o'-Fun." Most amusement park experts consider the Wall-o'-Fun to be the most popular ride currently in operation. It has been associated with three fatalities.

"My dad loved life and it really loved him back," said Wallace Gilfeather-Yez, Jr. In addition to his son, Yez's survivors include a daughter, LinLin Gilfeather-Yez, and two grandchildren. His wife, Imogene Gilfeather, a former undercover agent, died in February, of a severe case of everything.

CORRECTION: Imogene Gilfeather was not an undercover agent. She designed underwear. In 2002, her company, Featherware, acquired Down There, Limited. Renamed Featherdown Under, the concern, at the time of Imogene Gilfeather-Yez's death, was the twenty-seventh-largest maker of thongs in the underwear-wearing world.

END HERE

INDEX

SPECIAL BONUS EDITION
FOR READERS WHO HAVE
HAD LASIK SURGERY

A MESSAGE FROM THE PUBLISHER

Because it is our goal to publish books that have the maximal satisfaction quotient, we would like to hear from you, the reader. Please take the time to fill out the survey below so we know how we may better serve you.

1. In which of our other titles would you like to see Wally Yez make an appearance?

2. "I was never surprised by the page numbers."

   ( ) strongly agree

   ( ) somewhat agree

   ( ) neither agree or disagree

   ( ) somewhat disagree

   ( ) strongly disagree

3. Did you feel there were enough truths in this book? Be honest.

4. Did you like the food written about by this author? Will you be preparing any of it?

5. In your opinion, were there enough semi-colons on the pages? Would you like to see more? Would you like to see the periods italicized?

6. In what ways did this book alter the way you relate to mohair?

7. Compare and contrast the themes in this book with the passage of the 1930 Smoot-Hawley Tariff Act.

8. Do you think this author deserves a Guggenheim Fellowship? If so, would you write her a recommendation by December 1st?

9. What time is it?

Hmm

This book was based on the *Aeneid,* loosely (but not anti-Hellenicly).

To Ms. Patricia Marx,

Our book club is reading your book. What's with all the empty space? One of our members thinks it's symbolic but most of us deplore it. It's a disgrace. You should be ashamed of yourself. People in other parts of the world are starving.

Hugs,

Amy H.

Hi!

So far I found three typos in your book! I found only two typos in the Stephen King book I just read. I'll let you know how many more I find in your book! Okay?

Best,

Ms. Lorrie Tobias

A FINAL WORD FROM THE PUBLISHER

Even before Patty finished telling this story, our offices were in receipt of a curiously great number of letters and e-mails from readers. In the spirit of openness and interactivity, we would like to share with you some of these communications:

Dear Patricia Marx,

Were you in Miss Sheanshang's third-grade class at Rydal Elementary? If so, I sat next to you. Thank you very much.

Lorinda ("Sharkie") Duenwald

To whom it may concern;

I got a defective copy of Patricia Marx's book. It contains patches of blankness. Please send me the missing words.

Gratefully,

Henry Kerrey

MORE FROM OUR MAILBAG

Dear Pat,

Guess what? I read the end of your book first, but it didn't wreck anything. Is that a literary device?

From a reader,

Cookie Kummer

Dear Author or Writer,

This is the first time I have ever written a letter to an author or writer. What is your position on estate taxes? Please reply ASAP.

Sarah Stuart

Dear Scribner,

Would you please send me a coupon for Featherware lingerie? I am a 34C (34D from December to March) and am looking for something in lace, preferably beige. Please enclose receipt.

Hazel Traister

Hey,

My mother made me read your book. She accidentally bought two copies. IMHO, it is underrated. Thank you.

Matt Stine

Dear P. Marx,

Would you be interested in doing a reading at the Barnes & Noble in Coal Run Village, Kentucky, on October 31? If so, would you please not read aloud chaplettes 3, 12, 13, 25, 28, first half of 91, 211–242, and any portion of the book that talks about red meat?

Yours truly,

A. Aaron Radlauer

TO WHOM IT MAY CONCERN,
THIS ISN'T FRANCE!!!! IT'S SPELLED CHAPLET!!!!!!
MARK O'DONNELL

About the Author

Patricia Marx is a staff writer for *The New Yorker* and a former writer for *Saturday Night Live*. She is the author of several books, including the novel *Him Her Him Again The End of Him*, which was a finalist for the Thurber Prize for Humor. Marx was the first woman elected to the *Harvard Lampoon*. Starting in the fall of 2011, she will teach screenwriting at Princeton University. She can take a baked potato out of the oven with her bare hand.